Christopher Marlowe, Percy E. Pinkerton

The Dramatic Works of Christopher Marlowe

Christopher Marlowe, Percy E. Pinkerton

The Dramatic Works of Christopher Marlowe

ISBN/EAN: 9783337342432

Printed in Europe, USA, Canada, Australia, Japan

Cover: Foto ©Andreas Hilbeck / pixelio.de

More available books at **www.hansebooks.com**

THE DRAMATIC WORKS

OF

(SELECTED.)

𝔚𝔦𝔱𝔥 𝔞 𝔓𝔯𝔢𝔣𝔞𝔱𝔬𝔯𝔶 𝔑𝔬𝔱𝔦𝔠𝔢, 𝔅𝔦𝔬𝔤𝔯𝔞𝔭𝔥𝔦𝔠𝔞𝔩
𝔞𝔫𝔡 𝔊𝔯𝔦𝔱𝔦𝔠𝔞𝔩.

By PERCY E. PINKERTON.

𝔑𝔢𝔴 𝔜𝔬𝔯𝔨:

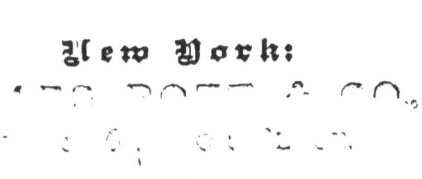

1885.

It is worthy of remark that "Dido" is Marlowe's only play which depends for its interest upon love. In all his other dramas he has never cared to give love any prominence. Nor did he try to create any interesting female figure. He has no heroines. Xenocrate, Zabina, Bellamira, Isabel, are all shadowy, intangible beings, without individuality, without charm. If "Dido" interests us, it is because Virgil has drawn her ; Marlowe merely reproduces the picture, with no perceptible sympathy for his subject. He seems to take most delight when he may indulge his passion for rich and coloured description ; when he may paint ships with golden cordage, crystal anchors, and ivory oars ; when he may speak of Dido's "silver arms" and "tears of pearl," or imagine "common soldiers" in "rich embroidered coats," with

"Silver whistles to control the winds."

And this exuberant passion for describing and contemplating the beautiful, this delight in all out- ward and visible loveliness, strong as it is in all his dramas, seems strongest in that magnificent

fragment of narrative verse, "Hero and Leander."
For its splendour of imagery, lustre of epithet, and
melody of phrase, this takes the first place among
all similar work of the golden Elizabethan age
Shakespeare's "Venus and Adonis" comes far below
it ; indeed, that poem is both an imitation and
failure. Marlowe handled the long rhyming couple
as no one else could handle it, giving to it the
three supreme qualities of simplicity, sensuousness
and passion. As we read his "goulden lynes," his
"sweet-according rimes," I think they touch or
imagination, they satisfy our sense of form and
melody in a far deeper degree than any dexterous
polished passage that we can choose from Pop
professedly a master in the making of that difficu
kind of verse.

To produce a match for "Hero and Leander,"
find an English poem really similar to it in feeling
and in form, we must pass down the centuries un
we come to that other "Elizabethan, born out
due time," until we come to Keats and to h'
"Endymion." That breathes the same frank, sen
suous love for the beautiful—that has the sam

THE JEW OF MALTA.

BARABAS BROODS UPON HIS WEALTH.

ACT I., SCENE 1.

Bara. So that of thus much that return was made ;
And of the third part of the Persian ships
There was the venture summ'd and satisfied.
As for those Sammites, and the men of Uz,
That bought my Spanish oils and wines of Greece,
Here have I purs'd their paltry silverlings.
Fie, what a trouble 'tis to count this trash !
Well fare the Arabians, who so richly pay
The things they traffic for with wedge of gold,
Whereof a man may easily in a day
Tell that which may maintain him all his life.
The needy groom, that never finger'd groat,
Would make a miracle of thus much coin ;
But he whose steel-barr'd coffers are cramm'd full,
And all his life-time hath been tired,
Wearying his fingers' ends with telling it,
Would in his age be loath to labour so,
And for a pound to sweat himself to death.

Give me the merchants of the Indian mines,
That trade in metal of the purest mould ;
The wealthy Moor, that in the eastern rocks
Without control can pick his riches up,
And in his house heap pearl like pebble-stones,
Receive them free, and sell them by the weight ;
Bags of fiery opals, sapphires, amethysts,
Jacinths, hard topaz, grass-green emeralds,
Beauteous rubies, sparkling diamonds,
And seld-seen costly stones of so great price,
As one of them, indifferently rated,
And of a carat of this quantity,
May serve, in peril of calamity,
To ransom great kings from captivity.
This is the ware wherein consists my wealth ;
And thus methinks should men of judgment frame
Their means of traffic from the vulgar trade,
And, as their wealth increaseth, so inclose
Infinite riches in a little room.
But now how stands the wind !
Into what corner peers my halcyon's bill ?
Ha ! to the east ? yes.   See how stand the vanes—
East and by south : why, then, I hope my ships
I sent for Egypt and the bordering isles
Are gotten up by Nilus' winding banks ;
Mine argosy from Alexandria,
Loaden with spice and silks, now under sail,
Are smoothly gliding down by Candy-shore
To Malta, through our Mediterranean sea.

THE JEW AND HIS DAUGHTER.

ACT II., SCENE 1.

Bara. Thus, like the sad-presaging raven, that tolls
The sick man's passport in her hollow beak,
And in the shadow of the silent night
Doth shake contagion from her sable wings,
Vex'd and tormented runs poor Barabas
With fatal curses towards these Christians.
The incertain pleasures of swift-footed time
Have ta'en their flight, and left me in despair ;
And of my former riches rests no more
But bare remembrance ; like a soldier's scar,
That has no further comfort for his maim.—
O, Thou, that with a fiery pillar ledd'st
The sons of Israel through the dismal shades,
Light Abraham's offspring ; and direct the hand
Of Abigail this night ! or let the day
Turn to eternal darkness after this !—
No sleep can fasten on my watchful eyes,
Nor quiet enter my distemper'd thoughts,
Till I have answer from my Abigail.
                              [*Enter* ABIGAIL *above.*
Abig. Now have I happily espied a time
To search the plank my father did appoint ;
And here, behold, unseen, where I have found
The gold, the pearls, and jewels, which he hid.
Bara. Now I remember those old women's words,
Who in my wealth would tell me winter's tales,
And speak of spirits and ghosts that glide by night
About the place were treasure hath been hid :
And now methinks that I am one of those ;

For, whilst I live, here lives my soul's sole hope,
And, when I die, here shall my spirit walk.

Abig. Now that my father's fortune were so
good
As but to be about this happy place !
'Tis not so happy : yet, when we parted last,
He said he would attend me in the morn.
Then, gentle Sleep, where'er his body rests.
Give charge to Morpheus that he may dream
A golden dream, and of the sudden wake,
Come and receive the treasure I have found.

Bara. Bueno para todos mi ganado no era :
As good go on, as sit so sadly thus. —
But stay : what star shines yonder in the east ?
The loadstar of my life, if Abigail. —
Who's there ?

Abig. Who's that ?

Bara. Peace, Abigail ! 'tis I.

Abig. Then, father, here receive thy happiness.

Bara. Hast thou't ?

Abig. Here. [*throws down bags*] Hast thou't ?
There's more, and more, and more.

Bara. O my girl,
My gold, my fortune, my felicity,
Strength to my soul, death to mine enemy ;
Welcome the first beginner of my bliss !
O Abigail, Abigail, that I had thee here too !
Then my desires were fully satisfied :
But I will practise thy enlargement thence :
O girl ! O gold ! O beauty ! O my bliss !
[*Hugs the bags.*

Abig. Father, it draweth towards midnight now,
And 'bout this time the nuns begin to wake ;
To shun suspicion, therefore, let us part.

Bara. Farewell, my joy, and by my fingers take
A kiss from him that sends it from his soul.

[*Exit* ABIGAIL *above.*

Now, Phœbus, ope the eyelids of the day,
And, for the raven, wake the morning lark,
That I may hover with her in the air,
Singing o'er these, as she does o'er her young.

THE JEW'S LESSON IN CHRISTIAN CHARITY.

ACT II., SCENE 2.

Bara. Now let me know thy name, and therewithal
Thy birth, condition, and profession.

Itha. Faith, sir, my birth is but mean ; my name's
Ithamore ; my profession what you please.

Bara. Hast thou no trade ? then listen to my words,
And I will teach [thee] that shall stick by thee :
First, be thou void of these affections,
Compassion, love, vain hope, and heartless fear ;
Be mov'd at nothing, see thou pity none,
But to thyself smile when the Christians moan.

Itha. O, brave master ! I worship your nose for this.

Bara. As for myself, I walk abroad o' nights,
And kill sick people groaning under walls :
Sometimes I go about and poison wells ;
And now and then, to cherish Christian thieves,
I am content to lose some of my crowns,
That I may, walking in my gallery,
See 'em go pinion'd along by my door.
Being young, I studied physic, and began
To practise first upon the Italian ;
There I enrich'd the priests with burials
And always kept the sexton's arms in ure

With digging graves and ringing dead men's knells :
And, after that, was I an engineer,
And in the wars 'twixt France and Germany,
Under pretence of helping Charles the Fifth,
Slew friend and enemy with my stratagems :
Then, after that, was I an usurer,
And with extorting, cozening, forfeiting,
And tricks belonging unto brokery,
I fill'd the gaols with bankrupts in a year,
And with young orphans planted hospitals ;
And every moon made some or other mad,
And now and then one hang himself for grief,
Pinning upon his breast a long great scroll
How I with interest tormented him.
But mark how I am blest for plaguing them—
I have as much coin as will buy the town.
But tell me now, how hast thou spent thy time ?
    Itha. Faith, master,
In setting Christian villages on fire,
Chaining of eunuchs, binding galley-slaves.
One time I was an hostler in an inn,
And in the night-time secretly would I steal
To travellers' chambers, and there cut their throats :
Once at Jerusalem, where the pilgrims kneel'd,
I strewèd powder on the marble stones,
And therewithal their knees would rankle so,
That I have laughed a-good to see the cripples
Go limping home to Christendom on stilts.
    Bara. Why, this is something : make account of me
As of thy fellow; we are villains both ;
Both circumcised ; we hate Christians both ;
Be true and secret ; thou shall want no gold.

THE MURDER OF THE FRIAR.

ACT IV., SCENE 2.

Enter BARABAS *and* ITHAMORE.

Bara. Ithamore, tell me, is the friar asleep?
Itha. Yes ; and I know not what the reason is,
Do what I can, he will not strip himself,
Nor go to bed, but sleeps in his own clothes :
I fear me he mistrusts what we intend.
Bara. No ; 'tis an order which the friars use :
Yet if he knew our meanings, could he scape ?
Itha. No, none can hear him, cry he ne'er so loud.
Bara. Why, true ; therefore did I place him there :
The other chambers open towards the street.
Itha. You loiter, master ; wherefore stay we thus ?
O, how I long to see him shake his heels !
Bara. Come on, sirrah :
Off with your girdle ; make a handsome noose.—
[ITHAMORE *takes off his girdle, and ties a noose on it.*
Friar, awake !
[*They put the noose round the* Friar's *neck.*
Friar Barn. What, do you mean to strangle me ?
Itha. Yes, 'cause you use to confess.
Bara. Blame not us, but the proverb—Confess and
be hanged.—Pull hard.
Friar Barn. What, will you have my life ?
Bara. Pull hard, I say.—You would have had my
    goods.
Itha. Ay, and our lives too—therefore pull amain.
[*They strangle the* Friar.
'Tis neatly done, sir ; here's no print at all.
Bara. Then is it as it should be. Take him up.

Itha. Nay, master, be ruled by me a little.   [*Takes the body, sets it upright against the wall, and puts a staff in its hand.*] So, let him lean upon his staff; excellent ! he stands as if he were begging of bacon.

Bara. Who would not think but that this friar
  liv'd ?
What time o' night is't now, sweet Ithamore !

Itha. Towards one.

Bara. Then will not Jacomo be long from hence.
            [*Exeunt.*

    Enter FRIAR JACOMO.

Friar Jac. This is the hour wherein I shall proceed ;
O happy hour, wherein I shall convert
An infidel, and bring his gold into our treasury !
But soft ! is not this Barnardine ? it is ;
And, understanding I should come this way,
Stands here o' purpose, meaning me some wrong,
And intercept my going to the Jew.—
Barnardine !
Wilt thou not speak ? thou think'st I see thee not ;
Away, I'd wish thee, and let me go by :
No, wilt thou not ? nay, then, I'll force my way ;
And, see, a staff stands ready for the purpose.
As thou lik'st that, stop me another time !
  [*Takes the staff, and strikes down the body.*

  Enter BARABAS *and* ITHAMORE.

Bara. Why, how now Jacomo ! what hast thou
  done ?

Friar Jac. Why, stricken him that would have
  struck at me.

Bara. Who is it! Barnardine! now, out, alas, he is slain!

Itha. Ay, master, he's slain; look how his brains drop out on's nose.

Friar Jac. Good sirs, I have done't: but nobody knows it but you two; I may escape.

Bara. So might my man and I hang with you for company.

Itha. No; let us bear him to the magistrates.

Friar Jac. Good Barabas, let me go.

Bara. No, pardon me; the law must have his course:
I must be forc'd to give in evidence,
That, being importun'd by this Barnardine
To be a Christian, I shut him out,
And there he sate: now I, to keep my word,
And give my goods and substance to your house,
Was up thus early, with intent to go
Unto your friary, because you stay'd.

Itha. Fie upon 'em! master, will you turn Christian,
when holy friars turn devils and murder one another?

Bara. No; for this example I'll remain a Jew:
Heaven bless me! what, a friar a murderer!
When shall you see a Jew commit the like?

Itha. Why, a Turk could ha' done no more.

Bara. To-morrow is the sessions; you shall to it.—
Come, Ithamore, let's help to take him hence.

Friar Jac. Villains, I am a sacred person; touch me not.

Bara. The law shall touch you; we'll but lead you, we:
'Las, I could weep at your calamity!—
Take in the staff too, for that must be shown:
Law wills that each particular be known.   [*Exeunt.*

THE JEW, IN DISGUISE, POISONS HIS TRUANT SLAVE.

Act IV., Scene 5.

Bell. A French musician !—Come, let's hear your skill.

Bara. Must tuna my lute for sound, twang, twang, first.

Itha. Wilt drink, Frenchman ? here's to thee with a——Pox on this drunken hiccup !

Bara. Gramercy, monsieur.

Bell. Prithee, Pilia-Borza, bid the fiddler give me the posy in his hat there.

Pilia. Sirrah, you must give my mistress your posy.

Bara. A votre commandement, madame.

[*Giving noscgay.*

Bell. How sweet, my Ithamore, the flowers smell !

Itha. Like thy breath, sweetheart ; no violet like 'em.

Pilia. Foh ! methinks they stink like a hollyhock.

Bara. So, now I am reveng'd upon 'em all :
The scent thereof was death ; I poison'd it.   [*Aside.*

Itha. Play, fiddler, or I'll cut your cat's guts into chitterlings.

Bara. Pardonnez moi, be no in tune yet : so, now, now all be in.

Itha. Give him a crown, and fill me out more wine.

Pilia. There's two crowns for thee : play.

[*Giving money.*

Bara. How liberally the villain gives me mine own gold !   [*Aside, and then plays.*

Pilia. Methinks he fingers very well.

Bara. So did you when you stole my gold.   [*Aside.*

Pilia. How swift he runs !

Bara. You run swifter when you threw my gold out of my window. [*Aside.*

Bell. Musician, hast been in Malta long !

Bara. Two, three, four month, madam.

Itha. Dost not know a Jew, one Barabas ?

Bara. Very mush ; monsieur, you no be his man ?

Pilia. His man !

Itha. I scorn the peasant ; tell him so.

Bara. He knows it already. [*Aside.*

Itha. 'Tis a strange thing of that Jew, he lives upon pickled grasshoppers and sauced mushrooms.

Bara. What a slave's this ! the governor feeds not as I do. [*Aside.*

Itha. He never put on clean shirt since he was circumcised.

Bara. Oh rascal ! I change myself twice a-day. [*Aside.*

Itha. The hat he wears, Judas left under the elder when he hanged himself.

Bara. 'Twas sent me for a present from the Great Cham. [*Aside.*

Pilia. A nasty slave he is.—Whither now, fiddler ?

Bara. *Pardonnez moi, monsieur ;* me be no well.

Pilia. Farewell, fiddler. [*Exit* BARABAS.] One letter more to the Jew.

Bell. Prithee, sweet love, one more, and write it sharp.

Itha. No, I'll send by word of mouth now.—Bid him deliver thee a thousand crowns, by the same token that the nuns loved rice, that Friar Barnardine slept in his own clothes ; any of 'em will do it.

Pilia. Let me alone to urge it, now I know the meaning.

Itha. The meaning has a meaning. Come, let's in : To undo a Jew is charity, and not sin.

EDWARD THE SECOND.

PERSONS REPRESENTED.

Edward II.
Edward III.
Gaveston.
Old Spencer.
Young Spencer
Earl Mortimer.
Young Mortimer.
Berkeley.
Lancaster.
Leicester.
Edmund, *Earl of Kent.*
Arundel.
Warwick.
Pembroke.
Archbishop of Canterbury.
Bishop of Winchester.
Bishop of Coventry.

Beaumont
Trussel.
Sir John Hainault.
Levune.
Baldock.
Matrevis.
Gurney.
Rice ap Howel.
Lightborn.
Abbot.
Lords, Messengers, Monks,
  James, *etc.*, *etc.*

Queen Isabella.
Niece to Edward II
Ladies.

ACT THE FIRST.

SCENE I.

Enter GAVESTON, *reading a letter from the king.*

Gav. My father is deceased ! Come, Gaveston,
And share the kingdom with thy dearest friend.
Ah ! words that make me surfeit with delight !

What greater bliss can hap to Gaveston,
Than live and be the favourite of a king !
Sweet prince, I come ; these, these thy amorous lines
Might have enforced me to have swum from France,
And like Leander, gasped upon the sand,
So thou would'st smile, and take me in thine arms.
The sight of London to my exiled eyes
Is as Elysium to a new-come soul ;
Not that I love the city, or the men,
But that it harbours him I hold so dear—
The king, upon whose bosom let me lie,
And with the world be still at enmity.
What need the arctic people love starlight,
To whom the sun shines both by day and night ?
Farewell base stooping to the lordly peers !
My knee shall bow to none but to the king.
As for the multitude, they are but sparks,
Raked up in embers of their poverty—
Tanti ; I'll fawn first on the wind
That glanceth at my lips, and flieth away
But how now, what are these ?

    Enter three poor Men.

 Men. Such as desire your worship's service.
 Gav. What canst thou do ?
 1 *Man.* I can ride.
 Gav. But I have no horse. What art thou ?
 2 *Man.* A traveller.
 Gav. Let me see—thou would'st do well
To wait at my trencher, and tell me lies at dinner-
  time ;
And as I like your discoursing, I'll have you.
And what art thou ?
 3 *Man.* A soldier, that hath served against the Scot.

Gav. Why, there are hospitals for such as you ;
I have no war ; and therefore, sir, be gone.
    3 Man. Farewell, and perish by a soldier's hand,
That would'st reward them with an hospital.
    Gav. Aye, aye, these words of his move me as much
As if a goose would play the porcupine,
And dart her plumes, thinking to pierce my breast.
But yet it is no pain to speak men fair ;
I'll flatter these, and make them live in hope. [*Aside.*
You know that I came lately out of France,
And yet I have not viewed my lord the king ;
If I speed well, I'll entertain you all.
    Omnes. We thank your worship.
    Gav. I have some business.   Leave me to myself.
    Omnes. We will wait here about the court. [*Exeunt.*
    Gav. Do ; these are not men for me ;
I must have wanton poets, pleasant wits,
Musicians, that with touching of a string
May draw the pliant king which way I please :
Music and poetry are his delight ;
Therefore I'll have Italian masks by night,
Sweet speeches, comedies, and pleasing shows ;
And in the day, when he shall walk abroad,
Like sylvan nymphs my pages shall be clad ;
My men, like satyrs grazing on the lawns,
Shall with their goat-feet dance the antic hay ;
Sometimes a lovely boy in Dian's shape,
With hair that gilds the water as it glides,
Crownets of pearl about his naked arms,
And in his sportful hands an olive-tree,
To hide those parts which men delight to see,
Shall bathe him in a spring ; and there, hard by,
One like Actæon, peeping through the grove,
Shall by the angry goddess be transform'd,

And running in the likeness of an hart,
By yelping hounds pull'd down, shall seem to die :
Such things as these best please his majesty.
By'r lord ! here comes the king and the nobles
From the parliament.   I'll stand aside.

Enter the KING, LANCASTER, MORTIMER, *senior,*
    MORTIMER, *junior,* EDMUND Earl of Kent, GUY
    Earl of Warwick, *etc.*

Edw. Lancaster !
Lan. My lord.
Gav. That Earl of Lancaster do I abhor.   [*Aside.*
Edw. Will you not grant me this ? In spite of them
I'll have my will ; and these two Mortimers,
That cross me thus, shall know I am displeased.
    E. Mor. If you love us, my lord, hate Gaveston.
    Gav. That villain Mortimer, I'll be his death !
                                                     [*Aside.*
    Y. Mor. Mine uncle here, this earl, and I myself,
Were sworn unto your father at his death,
That he should ne'er return into the realm :
And know, my lord, ere I will break my oath,
This sword of mine, that should offend your foes,
Shall sleep within the scabbard at thy need,
And underneath thy banners march who will,
For Mortimer will hang his armour up.
    Gav. Mort Dieu !   [*Aside.*
    Edw. Well, Mortimer, I'll make thee rue these
        words.
Beseems it thee to contradict thy king ?
Frown'st thou thereat, aspiring Lancaster ?
The sword shall plane the furrows of thy brows.
And hew these knees that now are grown so stiff.
                        (D)

I will have Gaveston ; and you shall know
What danger 'tis to stand against your king.
   Gav. Well done, Ned !   [*Aside.*
   Lan. My lord, why do you thus incense your peers,
That naturally would love and honour you
But for that base and obscure Gaveston ?
Four earldoms have I, besides Lancaster—
Derby, Salisbury, Lincoln, Leicester,
These will I sell, to give my soldiers pay,
Ere Gaveston shall stay within the realm ;
Therefore, if he be come, expel him straight.
   Edw. Barons and earls, your pride hath made me
      mute ;
But now I'll speak, and to the proof I hope.
I do remember, in my father's days,
Lord Piercy of the North, being highly moved,
Braved Moubery in presence of the king ;
For which, had not his highness loved him well,
He should have lost his head ; but with his look
The undaunted spirit of Piercy was appeased,
And Moubery and he were reconciled.
Yet dare you brave the king unto his face ;
Brother, revenge it, and let these their heads,
Preach upon poles, for trespass of their tongues.
   War. Oh, our heads !   [grant.—
   Edw. Aye, yours ; and therefore I would wish you
   War. Bridle thy anger, gentle Mortimer.
   Y. Mor. I cannot, nor I will not ; I must speak.
Cousin, our hands I hope shall fence our heads,
And strike off his that makes you threaten us.
Come, uncle, let us leave the brainsick king,
And henceforth parley with our naked swords.
   E. Mor. Wiltshire hath men enough to save our
      heads.

War. All Warwickshire will leave him for my sake.
Lan. And northward Lancaster hath many friends.
Adieu, my lord ; and either change your mind,
Or look to see the throne, where you should sit,
To float in blood ; and at thy wanton head,
The glozing head of thy base minion thrown.
[*Exeunt* Nobles.
Edw. I cannot brook these haughty menaces ;
Am I a king, and must be over-ruled ?
Brother, display my ensigns in the field ;
I'll bandy with the barons and the earls,
And either die or live with Gaveston.
Gav. I can no longer keep me from my lord.
[*Comes forward.*
Edw. What, Gaveston ! welcome—Kiss not my
hand—
Embrace me, Gaveston, as I do thee.
Why should'st thou kneel ? know'st thou not who I
am ?
Thy friend, thyself, another Gaveston !
Not Hylas was more mourned of Hercules,
Than thou hast been of me since thy exile.
Gav. And since I went from hence, no soul in hell
Hath felt more torment than poor Gaveston.
Edw. I know it—Brother, welcome home my friend.
Now let the treacherous Mortimers conspire,
And that high-minded Earl of Lancaster ;
I have my wish, in that I 'joy thy sight ;
And sooner shall the sea o'erwhelm my land,
Than bear the ship that shall transport thee hence.
I here create thee Lord High Chamberlain,
Chief Secretary to the state and me,
Earl of Cornwall, King and Lord of Man.
Gav. My lord, these titles far exceed my worth.

Kent. Brother, the least of these may well suffice
For one of greater birth than Gaveston.
  Edw. Cease, brother: for I cannot brook these words.
Thy worth, sweet friend, is far above my gifts,
Therefore, to equal it, receive my heart ;
If for these dignities thou be envied,
I'll give thee more ; for, but to honour thee,
Is Edward pleased with kingly regiment.
Fear'st thou thy person ? thou shalt have a guard.
Wantest thou gold ? go to my treasury.
Wouldst thou be loved and feared ? receive my seals :
Save or condemn, and in our name command
Whatso thy mind affects, or fancy likes.
  Gav. It shall suffice me to enjoy your love,
Which, whiles I have, I think myself as great
As Cæsar riding in the Roman street,
With captive kings at his triumphant car.

Enter the BISHOP OF COVENTRY.

  Edw. Whither goes my lord of Coventry so fast ?
  Bish. To celebrate your father's exequies.
But is that wicked Gaveston returned ?
  Edw. Aye, priest, and lives to be revenged on thee,
That wert the only cause of his exile.
  Gav. 'Tis true ; and but for reverence of these robes,
Thou should'st not plod one foot beyond this place.
  Bish. I did no more than I was bound to do ;
And, Gaveston, unless thou be reclaimed,
As then I did incense the parliament,
So will I now, and thou shalt back to France.
  Gav. Saving your reverence, you must pardon me.
  Edw. Throw off his golden mitre, rend his stole,
And in the channel christen him anew.

Kent. Ah, brother, lay not violent hands on him,
For he'll complain unto the see of Rome.
Gav. Let him complain unto the see of hell,
I'll be revenged on him for my exile.
Ewd. No, spare his life, but seize upon his goods :
Be thou lord bishop and receive his rents,
And make him serve thee as thy chaplain :
I give him thee—here, use him as thou wilt.
Gav. He shall to prison, and there die in bolts.
Edw. Aye, to the Tower, the Fleet, or where thou
wilt.
Bish. For this offence, be thou accurst of God !
Edw. Who's there ?   Convey this priest to the
Tower.
Bish. True, true.
Edw. But in the meantime, Gaveston, away,
And take possession of his house and goods.
Come, follow me, and thou shalt have my guard
To see it done, and bring thee safe again.
Gav. What should a priest do with so fair a house ?
A prison may best beseem his holiness.   [*Exeunt.*

SCENE II.

Enter both the MORTIMERS, WARWICK, *and* LANCASTER.
War. 'Tis true, the bishop is in the Tower,
And goods and body given to Gaveston.
Lan. What ! will they tyrannise upon the church ?
Ah, wicked king ! accursed Gaveston !
This ground, which is corrupted with their steps,
Shall be their timeless sepulchre or mine.
Y. Mor. Well, let that peevish Frenchman guard
him sure ;
Unless his breast be sword-proof he shall die.
E. Mor. How now, why droops the Earl of Lancaster ?

Y. Mor. Wherefore is Guy of Warwick discontent ?

Lan. That villain Gaveston is made an earl.

E. Mor. An earl !   [realm,

War. Aye, and besides Lord Chamberlain of the
And Secretary too, and Lord of Man.

E. Mor. We may not, nor we will not suffer this.

Y. Mor. Why post we not from hence to levy men ?

Lan. " My Lord of Cornwall," now at every word !
And happy is the man whom he vouchsafes,
For vailing of his bonnet, one good look.
Thus, arm-in-arm, the king and he doth march :
Nay more, the guard upon his lordship waits ;
And all the court begins to flatter him.

War. Thus leaning on the shoulder of the king,
He nods, and scorns, and smiles at those that pass.

E. Mor. Doth no man take exceptions at the slave ?

Lan. All stomach him, but none dare speak a word.

Y. Mor. Aye, that bewrays their baseness, Lan-
    caster.
Were all the earls and barons of my mind,
We'd hale him from the bosom of the king,
And at the court-gate hang the peasant up ;
Who, swoln with venom of ambitious pride,
Will be the ruin of the realm and us.

Enter the ARCHBISHOP OF CANTERBURY, *and a* Messenger.

War. Here comes my Lord of Canterbury's grace.

Lan. His countenance bewrays he is displeased.

Archbish. First were his sacred garments rent and
    torn,
Then laid they violent hands upon him ; next
Himself imprisoned, and his goods asseized :
This certify the pope—away, take horse.
                    [*Exit* Messenger.

Lan. My lord, will you take arms against the king?
Archbish. What need I? God himself is up in arms,
When violence is offered to the church.
    Y. Mor. Then will you join with us, that be his
    peers,
To banish or behead that Gaveston?
    Archbish. What else, my lords? for it concerns me
    near—
The bishoprick of Coventry is his.

Enter QUEEN ISABELLA.

    Y. Mor. Madam, whither walks your majesty so
    fast?
    Queen. Unto the forest, gentle Mortimer,
To live in grief and baleful discontent;
For now, my lord, the king regards me not,
But doats upon the love of Gaveston.
He claps his cheek, and hangs about his neck,
Smiles in his face, and whispers in his ears;
And when I come he frowns, as who should say,
" Go whither thou wilt, seeing I have Gaveston."
    E. Mor. Is it not strange, that he is thus bewitched?
    Y. Mor. Madam, return unto the court again:
That sly inveigling Frenchman we'll exile,
Or lose our lives; and yet ere that day come
The king shall lose his crown; for we have power,
And courage too, to be revenged at full.   [king.
    Archbish. But yet lift not your swords against the
    Lan. No; but we will lift Gaveston from hence.
    War. And war must be the means, or he'll stay still.
    Queen. Than let him stay; for rather than my lord
Shall be oppressed with civil mutinies,
I will endure a melancholy life,
And let him frolic with his minion.

Archbish. My lords, to ease all this, but hear me
     speak :—
We and the rest, that are his counsellors,
Will meet, and with a general consent
Confirm his banishment with our hands and seals.
     Lan. What we confirm the king will frustrate.
     Y. Mor. Then may we lawfully revolt from him.
     War. But say, my lord, where shall this meeting be?
     Archbish. At the New Temple.
     Y. Mor. Content.
     Archbish. And, in the meantime, I'll entreat you all
To cross to Lambeth, and there stay with me.
     Lan. Come then, let's away.
     Y. Mor. Madam, farewell !
     Queen. Farewell, sweet Mortimer ; and, for my sake,
Forbear to levy arms against the king.
     Y. Mor. Aye, if words will serve, if not, I must.
                              [*Exeunt.*

Scene III.

Enter Gaveston *and the* Earl of Kent.

Gav. Edmund, the mighty prince of Lancaster,
That hath more earldoms than an ass can bear,
And both the Mortimers, two goodly men,
With Guy of Warwick, that redoubted knight,
Are gone toward London—there let them remain.
                              [*Exeunt.*

Scene IV.

Enter Nobles, *and the* Archbishop of Canterbury.

Lan. Here is the form of Gaveston's exile :
May it please your lordship to subscribe your name.
Archbish. Give me the paper.
               [*He subscribes, as the others do after him.*

Lan. Quick, quick, my lord ; I long to write my name.

War. But I long more to see him banished hence.

Y. Mor. The name of Mortimer shall fright the king,

Unless he be declined from that base peasant.

Enter the KING, GAVESTON, *and* KENT.

Edw. What, are you moved that Gaveston sits here ?
It is our pleasure, and we will have it so.

Lan. Your grace doth well to place him by your side,

For nowhere else the new earl is so safe.

E. Mor. What man of noble birth can brook this sight ?

Quam male conveniunt!

See what a scornful look the peasant casts !

Pem. Can kingly lions fawn on creeping ants ?

War. Ignoble vassal, that like Phaëton
Aspir'st unto the guidance of the sun.

Y. Mor. Their downfall is at hand, their forces down :

We will not thus be faced and over-peered.

Edw. Lay hands on that traitor Mortimer !

Y. Mor. Lay hands on that traitor Gaveston !

Kent. Is this the duty that you owe your king ?

War. We know our duties—let him know his peers.

Edw. Whither will you bear him ?   Stay, or ye shall die.

E. Mor. We are no traitors ; therefore threaten not.

Gav. No, threaten not, my lord, but pay them home !

Were I a king ——

Y. Mor. Thou villain, wherefore talk'st thou of a
    king,
That hardly art a gentleman by birth ?
Edw. Were he a peasant, being my minion,
I'll make the proudest of you stoop to him.
Lan. My lord, you may not thus disparage us.
Away, I say, with hateful Gaveston.
E. Mor. And with the Earl of Kent that favours him.
         [Attendants *remove* KENT *and* GAVESTON.
Edw. Nay, then, lay violent hands upon your king,
Here, Mortimer, sit thou in Edward's throne :
Warwick and Lancaster, wear you my crown :
Was ever king thus over-ruled as I !
Lan. Learn then to rule us better, and the realm.
Y. Mor. What we have done, our heart blood shall
    maintain,
War. Think you that we can brook this upstart
    pride ?
Edw. Anger and wrathful fury stops my speech.
Archbish. Why are you moved ? be patient, my lord,
And see what we your counsellors have done.
Y. Mor. My lords, now let us all be resolute,
And either have our wills or lose our lives.
Edw. Meet you for this ? proud, over-daring peers !
Ere my sweet Gaveston shall part from me,
This isle shall fleet upon the ocean,
And wander to the unfrequented Inde.
Archbish. You know that I am legate to the pope ;
On your allegiance to the see of Rome,
Subscribe, as we have done, to his exile.
Y. Mor. Curse him, if he refuse ; and then may we
Depose him and elect another king.
Edw. Aye, there it goes—but yet I will not yield.
Curse me, depose me, do the worst you can.

Lan. Then linger not, my lord, but do it straight.
Archbish. Remember how the bishop was abused !
Either banish him that was the cause thereof,
Or I will presently discharge these lords
Of duty and allegiance due to thee.
 Edw. It boots me not to threat—I must speak fair :
              [*Aside.*
The legate of the pope will be obeyed.
My lord, you shall be Chancellor of the realm ;
Thou, Lancaster, High Admiral of the fleet ;
Young Mortimer and his uncle shall be earls ;
And you, Lord Warwick, President of the North ;
And thou of Wales. If this content you not,
Make several kingdoms of this monarchy,
And share it equally amongst you all,
So I may have some nook or corner left,
To frolic with my dearest Gaveston.
 Archbish. Nothing shall alter us—we are resolved.
 Lan. Come, come, subscribe.
 Y. Mor. Why should you love him whom the
  world hates so ?
 Edw. Because he loves me more than all the world.
Ah, none but rude and savage-minded men
Would seek the ruin of my Gaveston !
You that are noble-born should pity him.
 War. You that are princely-born should shake
  him off :
For shame, subscribe, and let the lown depart.
 E. Mor. Urge him, my lord.
 Archbish. Are you content to banish him the
  realm ?
 Edw. I see I must, and therefore am content :
Instead of ink, I'll write it with my tears. [*Subscribes.*
 Y. Mor. The king is love-sick for his minion.

Edw. 'Tis done: and now, accursed hand, fall
        off !
Lan. Give it me: I'll have it published in the
        streets.
Y. Mor. I'll see him presently despatched away.
Archbish. Now is my heart at ease.
War. And so is mine.
Pem. This will be good news to the common sort.
E. Mor. Be it or no, he shall not linger here.
                [*Exeunt all except* KING EDWARD.
Edw. How fast they run to banish him I love !
They would not stir, were it to do me good.
Why should a king be subject to a priest ?
Proud Rome, that hatchest such imperial grooms,
With these thy superstitious taper lights,
Wherewith thy antichristian churches blaze,
I'll fire thy crazèd buildings, and enforce
The papal towers to kiss the lowly ground !
With slaughtered priests make Tiber's channel swell,
And banks rise higher with their sepulchres !
As for the peers, that back the clergy thus,
If I be king, not one of them shall live.

                Re-enter GAVESTON.

Gav. My lord, I hear it whispered every where
That I am banished, and must fly the land.
Edw. 'Tis true, sweet Gaveston : Oh, were it false
The legate of the Pope will have it so,
And thou must hence, or I shall be deposed,
But I will reign to be revenged of them ;
And therefore, sweet friend, take it patiently.
Live where thou wilt, I'll send thee gold enough ;
And long thou shalt not stay ; or, if thou dost,
I'll come to thee : my love shall ne'er decline.

Gav. Is all my hope turned to this hell of grief ?
Edw. Rend not my heart with thy too-piercing
words :
Thou from this land, I from myself am banished.
Gav. To go from hence grieves not poor Gaveston ;
But to forsake you, in whose gracious looks
The blessedness of Gaveston remains ;
For nowhere else seeks he felicity.
Edw. And only this torments my wretched soul,
That, whether I will or no, thou must depart.
Be governor of Ireland in my stead,
And there abide till fortune call thee home.
Here, take my picture, and let me wear thine :

[*They exchange pictures.*

O, might I keep thee here, as I do this,
Happy were I ! but now most miserable.
Gav. 'Tis something to be pitied of a king.
Edw. Thou shalt not hence—I'll hide thee,
Gaveston.
Gav. I shall be found, and then 'twill grieve me
more.
Edw. Kind words, and mutual talk makes our grief
greater ;
Therefore, with dumb embracement, let us part—
Stay, Gaveston, I cannot leave thee thus.
Gav. For every look, my love drops down a tear :
Seeing I must go, do not renew my sorrow.
Edw. The time is little that thou hast to stay,
And, therefore, give me leave to look my fill ;
But come, sweet friend, I'll bear thee on thy way.
Gav. The peers will frown.
Edw. I pass not for their anger—Come, let's go ;
O that we might as well return as go.

Enter KENT *and* QUEEN ISABEL.

Queen. Whither goes my lord?

Edw. Fawn not on me, French strumpet! get thee
gone.

Queen. On whom but on my husband should I
fawn?

Gav. On Mortimer! with whom, ungentle queen—
I say no more—judge you the rest, my lord.

Queen. In saying this, thou wrong'st me, Gaveston;
Is't not enough that thou corrupt'st my lord,
And art a bawd to his affections,
But thou must call mine honour thus in question?

Gav. I mean not so; your grace must pardon me.

Edw. Thou art too familiar with that Mortimer,
And by thy means is Gaveston exiled;
But I would wish thee reconcile the lords,
Or thou shalt ne'er be reconciled to me.

Queen. Your highness knows it lies not in my power.

Edw. Away, then! touch me not—Come, Gaveston.

Queen. Villain! 'tis thou that robb'st me of my
lord.

Gav. Madam, 'tis you that rob me of my lord.

Edw. Speak not unto her; let her droop and pine.

Queen. Wherein, my lord, have I deserved these
words?
Witness the tears that Isabella sheds,
Witness this heart, that, sighing for thee, breaks,
How dear my lord is to poor Isabel.

Edw. And witness heaven how dear thou art to me!
There weep; for till my Gaveston be repealed,
Assure thyself thou com'st not in my sight.
               [*Exeunt* EDWARD *and* GAVESTON.

Queen. O miserable and distressèd queen!

Would, when I left sweet France and was embarked,
That charming Circe, walking on the waves,
Had changed my shape, or that the marriage-day
The cup of Hymen had been full of poison,
Or with those arms that twined about my neck
I had been stifled, and not lived to see
The king my lord thus to abandon me !
Like frantic Juno will I fill the earth
With ghastly murmur of my sighs and cries ;
For never doated Jove on Ganymede
So much as he on cursed Gaveston ;
But that will more exasperate his wrath :
I must entreat him, I must speak him fair,
And be a means to call home Gaveston ;
And yet he'll ever doat on Gaveston :
And so am I for ever miserable.

Enter the NOBLES.

Lan. Look where the sister of the king of France
Sits wringing of her hands and beats her breast !
War. The king, I fear, hath ill-entreated her.
Pem. Hard is the heart that injures such a saint.
Y. Mor. I know 'tis 'long of Gaveston she weeps.
E. Mor. Why, he is gone.
Y. Mor. Madam, how fares your grace ?
Queen. Ah, Mortimer ! now breaks the king's hate
forth.
And he confesseth that he loves me not.
Y. Mor. Cry quittance, madam, then ; and love
not him.
Queen. No, rather will I die a thousand deaths ;
And yet I love in vain—he'll ne'er love me.
Lan. Fear ye not, madam ; now his minion's gone
His wanton humour will be quickly left.

Queen. Oh, never, Lancaster! I am enjoined
To sue upon you all for his repeal ;
This wills my lord, and this must I perform,
Or else be banished from his highness' presence.
　Lan. For his repeal, madam ! he comes not back,
Unless the sea cast up his shipwrecked body.
　War. And to behold so sweet a sight as that,
There's none here but would run his horse to death.
　Y. Mor. But, madam, would you have us call him
　　home ?
　Queen. Aye, Mortimer, for till he be restored,
The angry king hath banished me the court ;
And, therefore, as thou lov'st and tender'st me,
Be thou my advocate upon the peers.
　Y. Mor. What ! would you have me plead for
　　Gaveston ?
　E. Mor. Plead for him that will, I am resolved.
　Lan. And so am I, my lord ! dissuade the queen.
　Queen. O Lancaster ! let him dissuade the king,
For 'tis against my will he should return.
　War. Then speak not for him, let the peasant go.
　Queen. 'Tis for myself I speak, and not for him.
　Pem. No speaking will prevail, and therefore cease.
　Y. Mor. Fair queen, forbear to angle for the fish,
Which, being caught, strikes him that takes it dead ;
I mean that vile torpedo, Gaveston,
That now I hope floats on the Irish seas.
　Queen. Sweet Mortimer, sit down by me awhile,
And I will tell thee reasons of such weight,
As thou wilt soon subscribe to his repeal.
　Y. Mor. It is impossible ; but speak your mind.
　Queen. Then thus, but none shall hear it but our-
　　selves.

　　　　　　　　　　　[Talks to Y. Mor. *apart.*

Lan. My lords, albeit the queen win Mortimer,
Will you be resolute, and hold with me ?
E. Mor. Not I, against my nephew.
Pem. Fear not, the queen's words cannot alter him.
War. No, do but mark how earnestly she pleads.
Lan. And see how coldly his looks make denial.
War. She smiles, now for my life his mind is
    changed.
Lan. I'll rather lose his friendship I, than grant.
Y. Mor. Well, of necessity it must be so.
My lords, that I abhor base Gaveston
I hope your honours make no question,
And therefore, though I plead for his repeal,
'Tis not for his sake, but for our avail !
Nay, for the realm's behoof, and for the king's.
    Lan. Fie, Mortimer, dishonour not thyself !
Can this be true, 'twas good to banish him ?
And is this true, to call him home again ?
Such reasons made white black, and dark night day.
    Y. Mor. My lord of Lancaster, mark the respect.
Lan. In no respect can contraries be true.
Queen. Yet, good my lord, hear what he can allege.
War. All that he speaks is nothing, we are resolved.
 Y. Mor. Do you not wish that Gaveston were dead ?
Pem. I would he were.   [speak.
Y. Mor. Why then, my lord, give me but leave to
E. Mor. But, nephew, do not play the sophister.
 Y. Mor. This which I urge is of a burning zeal
To mend the king, and do our country good.
Know you not Gaveston hath store of gold,
Which may in Ireland purchase him such friends,
As he will front the mightiest of us all ?
And whereas he shall live and be beloved,
'Tis hard for us to work his overthrow.
        (E)

War. Mark you but that, my lord of Lancaster.
Y. Mor. But were he here, detested as he is,
How eas'ly might some base slave be suborned
To greet his lordship with a poniard,
And none so much as blame the murderer,
But rather praise him for that brave attempt,
And in the chronicle enrol his name
For purging of the realm of such a plague ?
  Pem. He saith true.
  Lan. Aye, but how chance this was not done before ?
  Y. Mor. Because, my lords, it was not thought
    upon :
Nay, more, when he shall know it lies in us
To banish him, and then to call him home,
'Twill make him vail the top-flag of his pride,
And fear to offend the meanest nobleman.
  E. Mor. But how if he do not, nephew ?
  Y. Mor. Then may we with some colour rise in
    arms !
For howsoever we have borne it out,
'Tis treason to be up against the king ;
So we shall have the people of our side,
Which for his father's sake lean to the king,
But cannot brook a night-grown mushroom,
Such a one as my lord of Cornwall is,
Should bear us down of the nobility.
And when the commons and the nobles join,
'Tis not the king can buckler Gaveston ;
We'll pull him from the strongest hold he hath.
My lords, if to perform this I be slack,
Think me as base a groom as Gaveston.
  Lan. On that condition, Lancaster will grant.
  War. And so will Pembroke and I.
  E. Mor. And I.

Y. Mor. In this I count me highly gratified,
And Mortimer will rest at your command.
Queen. And when this favour Isabel forgets,
Then let her live abandoned and forlorn.
But see, in happy time, my lord the king,
Having brought the Earl of Cornwall on his way,
Is new returned ; this news will glad him much ;
Yet not so much as me ; I love him more
Then he can Gaveston ; would he loved me
But half so much, then were I treble-blessed !

Enter KING EDWARD, *mourning.*

Edw. He's gone, and for his absence thus I mourn.
Did never sorrow go so near my heart,
As doth the want of my sweet Gaveston !
And could my crown's revenue bring him back,
I would freely give it to his enemies,
And think I gained, having bought so dear a friend.
Queen. Hark ! how he harps upon his minion.
Edw. My heart is as an anvil unto sorrow,
Which beats upon it like the Cyclops' hammers,
And with the noise turns up my giddy brain,
And makes me frantic for my Gaveston.
Ah ! had some bloodless fury rose from hell,
And with my kingly sceptre struck me dead,
When I was forced to leave my Gaveston !
Lan. Diablo ! what passions call you these ?
Queen. My gracious lord, I come to bring you news.
Edw. That you have parlèd with your Mortimer ?
Queen. That Gaveston, my lord, shall be repealed.
Edw. Repealed ! the news is too sweet to be true !
Queen. But will you love me, if you find it so ?
Edw. If it be so, what will not Edward do ?
Queen. For Gaveston, but not for Isabel.

Edw. For thee, fair queen, if thou lov'st Gaveston,
I'll hang a golden tongue about thy neck,
Seeing thou hast pleaded with so good success.
 Queen. No other jewels hang about my neck
Than these, my lord ; nor let me have more wealth
Than I may fetch from this rich treasury—
O how a kiss revives poor Isabel !
 Edw. Once more receive my hand ; and let this be
A second marriage 'twixt thyself and me.
 Queen. And may it prove more happy than the
  first !
My gentle lord, bespeak these nobles fair,
That wait attendance for a gracious look,
And on their knees salute your majesty.
 Edw. Courageous Lancaster, embrace thy king ;
And, as gross vapours perish by the sun,
Even so let hatred with thy sovereign's smile.
Live thou with me as my companion.
 Lan. This salutation overjoys my heart.
 Edw. Warwick shall be my chiefest counsellor :
These silver hairs will more adorn my court
Than gaudy silks, or rich embroidery.
Chide me, sweet Warwick, if I go astray.
 War. Slay me, my lord, when I offend your grace.
 Edw. In solemn triumphs, and in public shows,
Pembroke shall bear the sword before the king.
 Pem. And with this sword Pembroke will fight for
  you.
 Edw. But wherefore walks young Mortimer aside ?
Be thou commander of our royal fleet ;
Or if that lofty office like thee not,
I make thee here Lord Marshal of the realm.
 Y. Mor. My lord, I'll marshal so your enemies,
As England shall be quiet, and you safe.

Edw. And as for you, Lord Mortimer of Chirke,
Whose great achievements in our foreign war
Deserve no common place, nor mean reward ;
Be you the general of the levied troops,
That now are ready to assail the Scots.   [Inc,
   E. Mor. In this your grace hath highly honoured
For with my nature war doth best agree.
   Queen. Now is the king of England rich and strong,
Having the love of his renownèd peers.
   Edw. Aye, Isabel, ne'er was my heart so light.
Clerk of the crown, direct our warrant forth
For Gaveston to Ireland : [*Enter* BEAUMONT *with
   warrant.*] Beaumont, fly,
As fast as Iris, or Jove's Mercury.
   Bea. It shall be done, my gracious lord.
   Edw. Lord Mortimer, we leave you to your charge.
Now let us in, and feast it royally.
Against our friend the Earl of Cornwall comes
We'll have a general tilt and tournament ;
And then his marriage shall be solemnised.
For wot you not that I have made him sure
Unto our cousin, the Earl of Gloucester's heir ?
   Lan. Such news we hear, my lord.
   Edw. That day, if not for him, yet for my sake,
Who in the triumph will be challenger,
Spare for no cost ; we will requite your love.
   War. In this, or aught your highness shall command
   us.
   Edw. Thanks, gentle Warwick : come, let's in and
   revel.   [*Exeunt. Manent the* MORTIMERS.
   E. Mor. Nephew, I must to Scotland ; thou stayest
   here.
Leave now t' oppose thyself against the king :
Thou seest by nature he is mild and calm ;

And, seeing his mind so dotes on Gaveston,
Let him without controlment have his will.
The mightiest kings have had their minions:
Great Alexander loved Hephæstion,
The conquering Hercules for his Hylas wept,
And for Patroclus stern Achilles drooped:
And not kings only, but the wisest men;
The Roman Tully lov'd Octavius,
Grave Socrates wild Alcibiades.
Then let his grace, whose youth is flexible,
And promiseth as much as we can wish,
Freely enjoy that vain, light-headed earl;
For riper years will wean him from such toys.
　　Y. Mor. Uncle, his wanton humour grieves not
　　　　me;
But this I scorn, that one so basely-born
Should by his sovereign's favour grow so pert,
And riot it with the treasure of the realm.
While soldiers mutiny for want of pay,
He wears a lord's revenue on his back,
And, Midas-like, he jets it in the court,
With base outlandish cullions at his heels,
Whose proud fantastic liveries make such show,
As if that Proteus, god of shapes, appeared.
I have not seen a dapper Jack so brisk:
He wears a short Italian hooded cloak,
Larded with pearl, and in his Tuscan cap
A jewel of more value than the crown.
While others walk below, the king and he,
From out a window, laugh at such as we,
And flout our train, and jest at our attire.
Uncle, 'tis this makes me impatient.
　　E. Mor. But, nephew, now you see the king is
　　　　changed.

Y. Mor. Then so am I, and live to do him service :
But whilst I have a sword, a hand, a heart,
I will not yield to any such upstart.
You know my mind ; come, uncle, let's away.

[*Exeunt.*

ACT THE SECOND

Scene I.

Enter Young Spencer *and* Baldock.

Bald. Spencer,
Seeing that our lord the Earl of Gloucester's dead,
Which of the nobles dost thou mean to serve ?
Y. Spen. Not Mortimer, nor any of his side ;
Because the king and he are enemies.
Baldock, learn this of me, a factious lord
Shall hardly do himself good, much less us ;
But he that hath the favour of a king,
May with one word advance us while we live :
The liberal Earl of Cornwall is the man
On whose good fortune Spencer's hope depends.
Bald. What, mean you then to be his follower?
Y. Spen. No, his companion ; for he loves me
well,
And would have once preferred me to the king.
Bald. But he is banished ; there's small hope of
him.
Y. Spen. Aye, for a while ; but Baldock, mark the
end.
A friend of mine told me in secrecy
That he's repealed, and sent for back again ;
And even now a post came from the court
With letters to our lady from the king ;

And as she read she smiled, which makes me think
It is about her lover Gaveston.
    Bald. 'Tis like enough ; for since he was exiled
She neither walks abroad, nor comes in sight.
But I had thought the match had been broke off,
And that his banishment had changed her mind.
    Y. Spen. Our lady's first love is not wavering ;
My life for thine she will have Gaveston.
    Bald. Then hope I by her means to be preferred,
Having read unto her since she was a child.   [off.
    Y. Spen. Then, Baldock, you must cast the scholar
And learn to court it like a gentleman.
'Tis not a black coat and a little band,
A velvet caped cloak, faced before with serge,
And smelling to a nosegay all the day,
Or holding of a napkin in your hand,
Or saying a long grace at a table's end,
Or making low legs to a nobleman,
Or looking downward with your eyelids close,
And saying, "Truly, an't may please your honour,"
Can get you any favour with great men :
You must be proud, bold, pleasant, resolute,
And now and then stab, as occasion serves.
    Bald. Spencer, thou know'st I hate such formal
        toys,
And use them but of mere hypocrisy.
Mine old lord while he lived was so precise,
That he would take exceptions at my buttons,
And being like pins' heads, blame me for the bigness ;
Which made me curate-like in mine attire,
Though inwardly licentious enough,
And apt for any kind of villainy.
I am none of these common pedants, I,
That cannot speak without *propterea quod.*

Y. Spen. But one of those that saith, *quandoquidem,*
And hath a special gift to form a verb.
Bald. Leave off this jesting, here my lady comes.

Enter the LADY.

Lady. The grief for his exile was not so much,
As is the joy of his returning home.
This letter came from my sweet Gaveston :
What need'st thou, love, thus to excuse thyself ?
I know thou couldst not come and visit me :
I will not long be from thee, though I die. [*Reads.*
This argues the entire love of my lord ;
When I forsake thee, death seize on my heart :
[*Reads.*
But stay thee here where Gaveston shall sleep.
Now to the letter of my lord the king.—
He wills me to repair unto the court,
And meet my Gaveston ? why do I stay,
Seeing that he talks thus of my marriage-day ?
Who's there ?   Baldock !
See that my coach be ready, I must hence.
Bald. It shall be done, madam. [*Exit.*
Lady. And meet me at the park-pale presently.
Spencer, stay you and bear me company,
For I have joyful news to tell thee of ;
My lord of Cornwall is a coming over,
And will be at the court as soon as we.
Spen. I knew the king would have him home again.
Lady. If all things sort out, as I hope they will,
Thy service, Spencer, shall be thought upon.
Spen. I humbly thank your ladyship.
Lady. Come, lead the way ; I long till I am th're.
[*Exeunt.*

Scene II.

Enter Edward, *the* Queen, Lancaster, Young
Mortimer, Warwick, Pembroke, Kent, *and*
Attendants.

Edw. The wind is good, I wonder why he stays ;
I fear me he is wrecked upon the sea.
Queen. Look, Lancaster, how passionate he is,
And still his mind runs on his minion !
Lan. My lord.
Edw. How now ! what news ? is Gaveston arrived ?
Y. Mor. Nothing but Gaveston ! what means your
    grace ?
You have matters of more weight to think upon ;
The King of France sets foot in Normandy.
Edw. A trifle ! we'll expel him when we please.
But tell me, Mortimer, what's thy device
Against the stately triumph we decreed ?
Y. Mor. A homely one, my lord, not worth the
    telling.
Edw. Pray thee let me know it.
Y. Mor. But, seeing you are so desirous, thus it is :
A lofty cedar-tree, fair flourishing,
On whose top-branches kingly eagles perch,
And by the bark a canker creeps me up,
And gets into the highest bough of all :
The motto, *Æque tandem.*
Edw. And what is yours, my lord of Lancaster ?
Lan. My lord, mine's more obscure than Mortimer's.
Pliny reports there is a flying fish
Which all the other fishes deadly hate,
And therefore, being pursued, it takes the air :
No sooner is it up, but there's a fowl

That seizeth it : this fish, my lord, I bear,
The motto this : *Undique mors est.*
Kent. Proud Mortimer ! ungentle Lancaster !
Is this the love you bear your sovereign ?
Is this the fruit your reconcilement bears ?
Can you in words make show of amity,
And in your shields display your rancorous minds ?
What call you this but private libelling
Against the Earl of Cornwall and my brother ?
    Queen. Sweet husband, be content, they all love
    you.
    Edw. They love me not that hate my Gaveston.
I am that cedar, shake me not too much ;
And you the eagles ; soar ye ne'er so high,
I have the jesses that will pull ye down ;
And *Æque tandem* shall that canker cry
Unto the proudest peer of Britainy.
Though thou compar'st him to a flying fish,
And threatenest death whether he rise or fall,
'Tis not the hugest monster of the sea,
Nor foulest harpy that shall swallow him.
    Y. Mor. If in his absence thus he favours him,
What will he do whenas he shall be present ?
    Lan. That shall we see ; look where his lordship
comes.

        Enter GAVESTON.

    Edw. My Gaveston ! welcome to Tynemouth ! welcome to thy friend !
Thy absence made me droop and pine away ;
For, as the lovers of fair Danae,
When she was locked up in a brazen tower,
Desired her more, and waxed outrageous,
So did it fare with me ; and now thy sight

Is sweeter far than was thy parting hence
Bitter and irksome to my sobbing heart.
   Gav. Sweet lord and king, your speech preventeth
      mine,
Yet have I words left to express my joy :
The shepherd nipt with biting winter's rage
Frolics not more to see the painted spring,
Than I do to behold your majesty.
   Edw. Will none of you salute my Gaveston ?
   Lan. Salute him ? yes ; welcome Lord Chamberlain !
   Y. Mor. Welcome is the good Earl of Cornwall !
   War. Welcome, Lord Governor of the Isle of Man !
   Pem. Welcome, Master Secretary !
   Kent. Brother, do you hear them ?
   Edw. Still will these earls and barons use me thus.
   Gav. My lord, I cannot brook these injuries.
   Queen. Ah me ! poor soul, when these begin to jar.
                                  [Aside.
   Edw. Return it to their throats, I'll be thy warrant.
   Gav. Base, leaden earls, that glory in your birth,
Go sit at home and eat your tenants' beef ;
And come not here to scoff at Gaveston,
Whose mounting thoughts did never creep so low
As to bestow a look on such as you.
   Lan. Yet I disdain not to do this for you. *[Draws.*
   Edw. Treason ! treason ! where's the traitor ?
   Pem. Here ! here ! king :
Convey hence Gaveston ; they'll murder him.
   Gav. The life of thee shall salve this foul disgrace.
   Y. Mor. Villain ! thy life, unless I miss mine aim.
                        [Offers to stab him.
   Queen. Ah ! furious Mortimer, what hast thou done ?
   Y. Mor. No more than I would answer, were he
      slain.   *[Exit* GAVESTON, *with* Attendants.

    Edw. Yes, more than thou canst answer, though
      he live ;
Dear shall you both abide this riotous deed.
Out of my presence ! come not near the court.
    Y. Mor. I'll not be barred the court for Gaveston.
    Lan. We'll hale him by the ears unto the block.
    Edw. Look to your heads ; his is sure enough.
    War. Look to your own crown, if you back him thus.
    Kent. Warwick, these words do ill beseem thy years.
    Edw. Nay, all of them conspire to cross me thus ;
But if I live, I'll tread upon their heads
That think with high looks thus to tread me down.
Come, Edmund, let's away and levy men,
'Tis war that must abate these barons' pride.
              [*Exeunt the* KING, QUEEN, *and* KENT.
    War. Let's to our castles, for the king is moved.
    Y. Mor. Moved may he be, and perish in his wrath !
    Lan. Cousin, it is no dealing with him now,
He means to make us stoop by force of arms ;
And therefore let us jointly here protest,
To prosecute that Gaveston to the death.
    Y. Mor. By heaven, the abject villain shall not
      live !
    War. I'll have his blood, or die in seeking it.
    Pem. The like oath Pembroke takes.
    Lan. And so doth Lancaster.
Now send our heralds to defy the king ;
And make the people swear to put him down.

            Enter MESSENGER.

    Y. Mor. Letters ! from whence ?
    Mess. From Scotland, my lord.
             [*Giving letters to* MORTIMER.
    Lan. Why, how now, cousin, how fare all our friends?

Y. Mor. My uncle's taken prisoner by the Scots.
Lan. We'll have him ransomed, man ; be of good
    cheer.   [*pound.*
Y. Mor. They rate his ransom at five thousand
Who should defray the money but the king,
Seeing he is taken prisoner in his wars ?
I'll to the king.
Lan. Do, cousin, and I'll bear thee company.
War. Meantime, my lord of Pembroke and myself
Will to Newcastle here, and gather head.
Y. Mor. About it then, and we will follow you.
Lan. Be resolute and full of secrecy.
War. I warrant you.   [*Exit with* PEMBROKE.
Y. Mor. Cousin, and if he will not ransom him,
I'll thunder such a peal into his ears,
As never subject did unto his king.
Lan. Content, I'll bear my part—Holloa ! who's
    there ?   [GUARD *appears.*

Enter GUARD.

Y. Mor. Aye, marry, such a guard as this doth well.
Lan. Lead on the way.
Guard. Whither will your lordships ?
Y. Mor. Whither else but to the king.
Guard. His highness is disposed to be alone.
Lan. Why, so he may, but we will speak to him.
Guard. You may not in, my lord.
Y. Mor. May we not ?

Enter EDWARD *and* KENT.

Edw. How now ! what noise is this ?
Who have we there, is't you ?   [*Going.*
Y. Mor. Nay, stay, my lord, I come to bring you news ;
Mine uncle's taken prisoner by the Scots.

Edw. Then ransom him.

Lan. 'Twas in your wars ; you should ransom him.

Y. Mor. And you shall ransom him, or else——

Kent. What ! Mortimer, you will not threaten him ?

Edw. Quiet yourself, you shall have the broad seal,
To gather for him thoroughout the realm.

Lan. Your minion Gaveston hath taught you this.

Y. Mor. My lord, the family of the Mortimers
Are not so poor, but, would they sell their land,
'Twould levy men enough to anger you.
We never beg, but use such prayers as these.

Edw. Shall I still be haunted thus !

Y. Mor. Nay, now you're here alone, I'll speak
  my mind.

Lan. And so will I ; and then, my lord, farewell.

Y. Mor. The idle triumphs, masks, lascivious shows,
And prodigal gifts bestow'd on Gaveston,
Have drawn thy treasury dry, and made thee weak ;
The murmuring commons, overstretchèd, break.

Lan. Look for rebellion, look to be deposed :
Thy garrisons are beaten out of France,
And, lame and poor, lie groaning at the gates ;
The wild Oneyl, with swarms of Irish kerns,
Lives uncontrolled within the English pale ;
Unto the walls of York the Scots make road,
And, unresisted, drive away rich spoils.   [seas,

Y. Mor. The haughty Dane commands the narrow
While in the harbour ride thy ships unrigged.

Lan. What foreign prince sends thee ambassadors ?

Y. Mor. Who loves thee, but a sort of flatterers ?

Lan. Thy gentle queen, sole sister to Valois,
Complains that thou hast left her all forlorn.

Y. Mor. Thy court is naked, being bereft of those
That make a king seem glorious to the world—

I mean the peers, whom thou shouldst dearly love;
Libels are cast against thee in the street;
Ballads and rhymes made of thy overthrow.

    Lan. The northern borderers, seeing their houses
        burnt,
Their wives and children slain, run up and down,
Cursing the name of thee and Gaveston.

    Y. Mor. When wert thou in the field with banner
        spread,
But once: and then thy soldiers march'd like players,
With garish robes, not armour; and thyself,
Bedaub'd with gold, rode laughing at the rest,
Nodding and shaking of thy spangled crest,
Where women's favours hung like labels down.

    Lan. And thereof came it that the fleering Scots,
To England's high disgrace, have made this jig—
Maids of England, sore may you mourn,
For your lemans you have lost at Bannocksbourn—
With a heave and a ho!
What weeneth the King of England
So soon to have won Scotland?—
With a rombelow!

    Y. Mor. Wigmore shall fly, to set my uncle free.
    Lan. And, when 'tis done, our swords shall purchase
        more.
If you be mov'd, revenge it if you can:
Look next to see us with our ensigns spread.
                   [*Exeunt* NOBLES.

    Edw. My swelling heart for very anger breaks:
How oft have I been baited by these peers,
And dare not be revenged, for their power is great!
Yet, shall the crowing of these cockerels
Affright a lion? Edward, unfold thy paws,
And let their lives' blood slake thy fury's hunger.

If I be cruel and grow tyrannous,
Now let them thank themselves, and rue too late.
Kent. My lord, I see your love for Gaveston
Will be the ruin of the realm and you,
For now the wrathful nobles threaten wars,
And therefore, brother, banish him for ever.
Edw. Art thou an enemy to my Gaveston ?
Kent. Aye, and it grieves me that I favoured him.
Edw. Traitor, begone ! whine thou with Mortimer.
Kent. So will I, rather than with Gaveston.
Edw. Out of my sight, and trouble me no more !
Kent. No marvel though thou scorn thy noble peers,
When I, thy brother, am rejected thus.   [*Exit.*
Edw. Away !
Poor Gaveston, that has no friend but me.
Do what they can, we'll live in Tynemouth here,
And, so I walk with him about the walls,
What care I though the Earls begirt us round——
Here cometh she that's cause of all these jars.

Enter the QUEEN, *with* KING'S NIECE, *two* LADIES,
   GAVESTON, BALDOCK, *and* Young SPENCER.

Queen. My lord, 'tis thought the Earls are up in
   arms.
Edw. Aye, and 'tis likewise thought you favour
   them.
Queen. Thus do you still suspect me without cause ?
Lady. Sweet uncle ! speak more kindly to the
   queen.
Gav. My lord, dissemble with her, speak her fair.
Edw. Pardon me, sweet, I had forgot myself.
Queen. Your pardon is quickly got of Isabel.
Edw. The younger Mortimer is grown so brave,
That to my face he threatens civil wars.
            (F)

Gav. Why do you not commit him to the Tower?
Edw. I dare not, for the people love him well.
Gav. Why, then, we'll have him privily made away.
Edw. Would Lancaster and he had both caroused
A bowl of poison to each other's health !
But let them go, and tell me what are these ?
Lady. Two of my father's servants whilst he liv'd—
May't please your grace to entertain them now ?
Edw. Tell me, where wast thou born ?
What is thine arms ?
Bald. My name is Baldock, and my gentry
I fetch from Oxford, not from heraldry.
Edw. The fitter art thou, Baldock, for my turn.
Wait on me, and I'll see thou shalt not want.
Bald. I humbly thank your majesty.
Edw. Knowest thou him, Gaveston ?   [allied ;
Gav. Aye, my lord; his name is Spencer, he is well
For my sake, let him wait upon your grace ;
Scarce shall you find a man of more desert.
Edw. Then, Spencer, wait upon me ; for his sake
I'll grace thee with a higher style ere long.
Y. Spen. No greater titles happen unto me,
Than to be favoured of your majesty.
Edw. Cousin, this day shall be your marriage feast ;
And, Gaveston, think that I love thee well,
To wed thee to our niece, the only heir
Unto the Earl of Gloucester late deceased.
Gav. I know, my lord, many will stomach me,
But I respect neither their love nor hate.
Edw. The headstrong barons shall not limit me ;
He that I list to favour shall be great.
Come, let's away ; and when the marriage ends,
Have at the rebels, and their 'complices !
                                        [*Exeunt omnes.*

Scene III.

Enter Lancaster, Young Mortimer, Warwick,
Pembroke, *and* Kent.

Kent. My lords, of love to this our native land
I come to join with you and leave the king;
And in your quarrel and the realm's behoof
Will be the first that shall adventure life.

Lan. I fear me you are sent of policy,
To undermine us with a show of love.

War. He is your brother, therefore have we cause
To cast the worst, and doubt of your revolt.

Kent. Mine honour shall be hostage of my truth :
If that will not suffice, farewell, my lords.

Y. Mor. Stay, Edmund ; never was Plantagenet
False of his word, and therefore trust we thee.

Pem. But what's the reason you should leave him
now ?

Kent. I have informed the Earl of Lancaster.

Lan. And it sufficeth. Now, my lords, know this,
That Gaveston is secretly arrived,
And here in Tynemouth frolics with the king.
Let us with these our followers scale the walls,
And suddenly surprise them unawares.

Y. Mor. I'll give the onset.

War. And I'll follow thee.

Y. Mor. This tottered ensign of my ancestors,
Which swept the desert shore of that dead sea,
Whereof we got the name of Mortimer,
Will I advance upon this castle's walls.
Drums, strike alarum, raise them from their sport,
And ring aloud the knell of Gaveston !

Lan. None be so hardy as to touch the king ;
But neither spare you Gaveston nor his friends. [*Exeunt.*

Scene IV.

Enter the King *and* Spencer, *to them* Gaveston, *etc.*

Edw. O tell me, Spencer, where is Gaveston ?
Spen. I fear me, he is slain, my gracious lord.
Edw. No, here he comes ; now let them spoil and
kill.

Enter Queen, King's Niece, Gaveston, *and*
Nobles.

Fly, fly, my lords, the earls have got the hold,
Take shipping and away to Scarborough,
Spencer and I will post away by land.
    Gav. O stay, my lord, they will not injure you.
    Edw. I will not trust them ; Gaveston, away !
    Gav. Farewell, my lord.
    Edw. Lady, farewell.
    Lady. Farewell, sweet uncle, till we meet again.
    Edw. Farewell, sweet Gaveston ; and farewell,
niece.
    Queen. No farewell to poor Isabel thy queen ?
    Edw. Yes, yes, for Mortimer, your lover's sake.
                     [*Exeunt all but* Isabel.
    Queen. Heaven can witness I love none but you :
From my embracements thus he breaks away.
O that mine arms could close this isle about,
That I might pull him to me where I would !
Or that these tears, that drizzle from mine eyes,
Had power to mollify his stony heart,
That when I had him we might never part.

Enter the Barons. *Alarums.*

Lan. I wonder how he 'scaped !
Y. Mor. Who's this, the queen ?

Queen. Aye, Mortimer, the miserable queen,
Whose pining heart her inward sighs have blasted,
And body with continual mourning wasted :
These hands are tired with haling of my lord
From Gaveston, from wicked Gaveston,
And all in vain ; for, when I speak him fair,
He turns away, and smiles upon his minion.

 Y. Mor. Cease to lament, and tell us where's the
  king ?

 Queen. What would you with the king ? is't him
  you seek ?

 Lan. No, madam, but that cursed Gaveston.
Far be it from the thought of Lancaster,
To offer violence to his sovereign.
We would but rid the realm of Gaveston :
Tell us where he remains, and he shall die.

 Queen. He's gone by water unto Scarborough ;
Pursue him quickly and he cannot 'scape ;
The king hath left him, and his train is small.

 War. Forslow no time, sweet Lancaster, let's march.

 Y. Mor. How comes it that the king and he is
  parted ?

 Queen. That thus your army, going several ways,
Might be of lesser force : and with the power
That he intendeth presently to raise,
Be easily suppressed ; therefore be gone.

 Y. Mor. Here in the river rides a Flemish hoy ;
Let's all aboard, and follow him amain.

 Lan. The wind that bears him hence will fill our
  sails :
Come, come aboard, 'tis but an hour's sailing.

 Y. Mor. Madam, stay you within this castle here.

 Queen. No, Mortimer, I'll to my lord the king.

 Y. Mor. Nay, rather sail with us to Scarborough.

Queen. You know the king is so suspicious,
As if he hear I have but talked with you,
Mine honour will be called in question ;
And therefore, gentle Mortimer, be gone.
    Y. Mor. I cannot stay to answer you,
But think of Mortimer as he deserves.
                                        [*Exeunt* BARONS.
    Queen. So well hast thou deserved, sweet Mortimer,
As Isabel could live with thee for ever.
In vain I look for love at Edward's hand,
Whose eyes are fixed on none but Gaveston :
Yet once more I'll importune him with prayer.
If he be strange and not regard my words,
My son and I will over into France,
And to the king my brother there complain,
How Gaveston hath robbed me of his love :
But yet I hope my sorrows will have end,
And Gaveston this blessed day be slain.   [*Exit.*

SCENE V.

Enter GAVESTON, *pursued.*

    Gav. Yet, lusty lords, I have escaped your hands,
Your threats, your 'larums, and your hot pursuits ;
And though divorcèd from King Edward's eyes,
Yet liveth Pierce of Gaveston unsurprised,
Breathing, in hope (malgrado all your beards,
That muster rebels thus against your king)
To see his royal sovereign once again.

Enter the NOBLES.

    War. Upon him, soldiers, take away his weapons.
    Y. Mor. Thou proud disturber of thy country's
        peace,

Corrupter of thy king, cause of these broils,
Base flatterer, yield ! and were it not for shame,
Shame and dishonour to a soldier's name,
Upon my weapon's point here should'st thou fall,
And welter in thy gore.
    Lan. Monster of men !
That, like the Greekish strumpet, trained to arms
And bloody wars so many valiant knights ;
Look for no other fortune, wretch, than death !
King Edward is not here to buckler thee.
    War. Lancaster, why talk'st thou to the slave ?
Go, soldiers, take him hence, for by my sword
His head shall off : Gaveston, short warning
Shall serve thy turn. It is our country's cause,
That here severely we will execute
Upon thy person : hang him at a bough.
    Gav. My lords !——
    War. Soldiers, have him away ;
But for thou wert the favourite of a king,
Thou shalt have so much honour at our hands.
    Gav. I thank you all, my lords ; then I perceive,
That heading is one, and hanging is the other,
And death is all.

Enter EARL OF ARUNDEL.

    Lan. How now, my lord of Arundel ?
    Arun. My lords, King Edward greets you all by me.
    War. Arundel, say your message.
    Arun. His majesty, hearing you had taken Gaveston,
Intreateth you by me, but that he may
See him before he dies ; for why, he says,
And sends you word, he knows that die he shall ;
And if you gratify his grace so far,
He will be mindful of the courtesy.

War. How now ?

Gav. Renownèd Edward, how thy name
Revives poor Gaveston !

War. No, it needeth not ;
Arundel, we will gratify the king
In other matters ; he must pardon us in this.
Soldiers, away with him !

Gav. Why, my lord of Warwick,
Will not these delays beget my hopes ?
I know it, lords, it is this life you aim at,
Yet grant King Edward this.

Y. Mor. Shall thou appoint
What we shall grant ? Soldiers, away with him :
Thus we will gratify the king,
We'll send his head by thee ; let him bestow
His tears on that, for that is all he gets
Of Gaveston, or else his senseless trunk.

Lan. Not so, my lords, lest he bestow more cost
In burying him, than he hath ever earned.

Arun. My lords, it is his majesty's request,
And on the honour of a king he swears,
He will but talk with him, and send him back.

War. When, can you tell ? Arundel, no ; we wot,
He that the care of his re-alm remits,
And drives his nobles to these exigents
For Gaveston, will, if he sees him once,
Violate any promise to possess him.

Arun. Then if you will not trust his grace in
keep,
My lords, I will be pledge for his return.

Y. Mor. 'Tis honourable in thee to offer this ;
But for we know thou art a noble gentleman,
We will not wrong thee so, to make away
A true man for a thief.

Gav. How mean'st thou, Mortimer? this is over-
base.

Y. Mor. Away, base groom, robber of king's
renown,
Question with thy companions and mates.

Pem. My Lord Mortimer, and you, my lords, each
one,
To gratify the king's request therein,
Touching the sending of this Gaveston,
Because his majesty so earnestly
Desires to see the man before his death,
I will upon mine honour undertake
To carry him, and bring him back again ;
Provided this, that you my lord of Arundel
Will join with me.

War. Pembroke, what wilt thou do ?
Cause yet more bloodshed ?   Is it not enough
That we have taken him, but must we now
Leave him on "had I wist," and let him go ?

Pem. My lords, I will not over-woo your honours,
But if you dare trust Pembroke with the prisoner,
Upon mine oath, I will return him back.

Arun. My lord of Lancaster, what say you in
this ?

Lan. Why, I say, let him go on Pembroke's word.

Pem. And you, Lord Mortimer ?

Y. Mor. How say you, my lord of Warwick ?

War. Nay, do your pleasures, I know how 'twill
prove.

Pem. Then give him me.

Gav. Sweet sovereign, yet I come
To see thee ere I die.

War. Not yet, perhaps,
If Warwick's wit and policy prevail.   *Aside.*

Y. Mor. My lord of Pembroke, we deliver him to you ;
Return him on your honour.　Sound, away.

> [*Exeunt all but* PEMBROKE, ARUNDEL,
> GAVESTON, *and* Pembroke's men.

Pem. My lord [of Arundel], you shall go with me.
My house is not far hence—out of the way
A little, but our men shall go along.
We that have pretty wenches to our wives,
Sir, must not come so near to baulk their lips.

Arun. 'Tis very kindly spoke, my lord of Pembroke ;
Your honour hath an adamant of power
To draw a prince.

Pem. So, my lord.　Come hither, James.
I do commit this Gaveston to thee.
Be thou this night his keeper, in the morning
We will discharge thee of thy charge ; be gone !

Gav. Unhappy Gaveston, whither goest thou now !

> [*Exit with* Pembroke's men.

Horse-boy. My lord, we'll quickly be at Cobham.

> [*Exeunt.*

ACT THE THIRD.

SCENE I.

Enter GAVESTON, *mourning, and the* Earl of
Pembroke's men.

Gav. O treacherous Warwick ! thus to wrong thy
friend.

James. I see it is your life these arms pursue.

Gav. Weaponless must I fall, and die in bands ?
Oh ! must this day be period of my life ?
Centre of all my bliss !　An ye be men,
Speed to the king.

Enter WARWICK *and his company.*

War. My lord of Pembroke's men,
Strive you no more—I will have that Gaveston.
James. Your lordship doth dishonour to yourself,
And wrong our lord, your honourable friend.
War. No, James, it is my country's cause I follow.
Go, take the villain ; soldiers, come away,
We'll make quick work.   Commend   me   to   your
    master,
My friend, and tell him that I watched it well.
Come, let thy shadow parley with King Edward.
Gav. Treacherous earl, shall I not see the king ?
War. The king of heaven, perhaps, no other king.
Away !   [*Exeunt* WARWICK *and his* Men
                                with GAVESTON.
James. Come, fellows, it booted not for us to strive,
We will in haste go certify our lord.   [*Exeunt.*

SCENE II.

Enter KING EDWARD *and* Young SPENCER, BALDOCK,
and NOBLES *of the king's side, with drums and fifes.*

Edw. I long to hear an answer from the barons,
Touching my friend, my dearest Gaveston.
Ah ! Spencer, not the riches of my realm
Can ransom him ! ah, he is marked to die !
I know the malice of the younger Mortimer,
Warwick I know is rough, and Lancaster
Inexorable, and I shall never see
My lovely Pierce of Gaveston again !
The barons overbear me with their pride.
Y. Spen. Were I King Edward, England's sovereign,
Son to the lovely Eleanor of Spain,

Great Edward Longshanks' issue, would I bear
These braves, this rage, and suffer uncontrolled
These barons thus to beard me in my land,
In mine own realm ?   My lord, pardon my speech.
Did you retain your father's magnanimity,
Did you regard the honour of your name,
You would not suffer thus your majesty
Be counterbuft of your nobility.
Strike off their heads ; and let them preach on poles !
No doubt, such lessons they will teach the rest,
As by their preachments they will profit much,
And learn obedience to their lawful king.
      Edw. Yea, gentle Spencer, we have been too mild,
Too kind to them ; but now have drawn our sword,
And if they send me not my Gaveston,
We'll steel it on their crest, and poll their tops.
      Bald. This haught resolve becomes your majesty
Not to be tied to their affection,
As though your highness were a schoolboy still,
And must be awed and governed like a child.

Enter HUGH SPENCER, *father to the* Young SPENCER,
            with his truncheon and Soldiers.

      O. Spen. Long live my sovereign, the noble Edward,
In peace triumphant, fortunate in wars !
      Edw. Welcome, old man, com'st thou in Edward's
            aid ?
Then tell thy prince of whence, and what thou art.
      O. Spen. Lo, with a band of bowmen and of pikes,
Brown bills and targeteers, four hundred strong,
Sworn to defend King Edward's royal right,
I come in person to your majesty,
Spencer, the father of Hugh Spencer there,

Bound to your highness everlastingly,
For favour done, in him, unto us all.
  Edw. Thy father, Spencer?
  Y. Spen. True, an it like your grace,
That pours, in lieu of all your goodness shown,
His life, my lord, before your princely feet.
  Edw. Welcome ten thousand times, old man, again.
Spencer, this love, this kindness to thy king,
Argues thy noble mind and disposition.
Spencer, I here create thee Earl of Wiltshire,
And daily will enrich thee with our favour,
That, as the sunshine, shall reflect o'er thee.
Besides, the more to manifest our love,
Because we hear Lord Bruce doth sell his land,
And that the Mortimers are in hand withal,
Thou shalt have crowns of us t' outbid the barons :
And, Spencer, spare them not, [but] lay it on.
Soldiers, a largess, and thrice welcome all !
  Y. Spen. My lord, here comes the queen.

> *Enter the* QUEEN *and her* Son, *and* LEVUNE,
> *a Frenchman.*

  Edw. Madam, what news?
  Queen. News of dishonour, lord, and discontent.
Our friend Levune, faithful and full of trust,
Informeth us, by letters and by words,
That Lord Valois our brother, King of France,
Because your highness hath been slack in homage,
Hath seizèd Normandy into his hands.
These be the letters, this the messenger.
  Edw. Welcome, Levune.   Tush, Sib, if this be all,
Valois and I will soon be friends again.
But to my Gaveston : shall I never see,
Never behold thee more ?   Madam, in this matter

We will employ you and your little son ;
You shall go parley with the King of France.
Boy, see you bear you bravely to the king,
And do your message with a majesty.   [weight
   Prince. Commit not to my youth things of more
That fits a prince so young as I to bear,
And fear not, lord and father, heaven's great beams
On Atlas' shoulder shall not lie more safe,
Than shall your charge committed to my trust.
   Queen. Ah, boy ! this towardness makes thy mother
     fear
Thou art not marked to many days on earth.
   Edw. Madam, we will that you with speed be
     shipped,
And this our son ; Levune shall follow you
With all the haste we can despatch him hence.
Choose of our lords to bear you company ;
And go in peace, leave us in wars at home.
   Queen. Unnatural wars, where subjects brave their
     king ;
God end them once. My lord, I take my leave,
To make my preparation for France.
                  [*Exit with* PRINCE.

             Enter ARUNDEL.

   Edw. What, Lord Arundel, dost thou come alone ?
   Arun. Yea, my good lord, for Gaveston is dead.
   Edw. Ah, traitors ! have they put my friend to
     death ?
Tell me, Arundel, died he ere thou cam'st,
Or didst thou see my friend to take his death ?
   Arun. Neither, my lord ; for as he was surprised,
Begirt with weapons and with enemies round,
I did your highness' message to them all ;

Demanding him of them, entreating rather,
And said, upon the honour of my name,
That I would undertake to carry him
Unto your highness, and to bring him back.

Edw. And tell me, would the rebels deny me
that ?

Y. Spen. Proud recreants !

Edw. Yea, Spencer, traitors all.

Arun. I found them at first inexorable ;
The Earl of Warwick would not bide the hearing,
Mortimer hardly, Pembroke and Lancaster
Spake least : and when they flatly had denied,
Refusing to receive me pledge for him,
The Earl of Pembroke mildly thus bespake :
" My lords, because our sovereign sends for him,
And promiseth he shall be safe returned,
I will this undertake to have him hence,
And see him re-delivered to your hands."

Edw. Well, and how fortunes [it] that he came
not ?

Y. Spen. Some treason, or some villainy was the
cause.

Arun. The Earl of Warwick seized him on his
way ;
For being delivered unto Pembroke's men,
Their lord rode home thinking his prisoner safe ;
But ere he came, Warwick in ambush lay,
And bare him to his death ; and in a trench
Strake off his head, and marched unto the camp.

Y. Spen. A bloody part, flatly 'gainst law of
arms.

Edw. Oh shall I speak, or shall I sigh and die !

Y. Spen. My lord, refer your vengeance to the sword
Upon these barons ; hearten up your men ;

Let them not unrevenged murder your friends !
Advance your standard, Edward, in the field,
And march to fire them from their starting holes.
                                    [EDWARD *kneels.*
    Edw. By earth, the common mother of us all !
By heaven, and all the moving orbs thereof !
By this right hand ! and by my father's sword !
And all the honours 'longing to my crown !
I will have heads, and lives for him, as many
As I have manors, castles, towns, and towers. [*Rises.*
Treacherous Warwick ! traitorous Mortimer !
If I be England's king, in lakes of gore
Your headless trunks, your bodies will I trail,
That you may drink your fill, and quaff in blood,
And stain my royal standard with the same,
That so my bloody colours may suggest
Remembrance of revenge immortally
On your accursèd traitorous progeny,
You villains, that have slain my Gaveston !
And in his place of honour and of trust,
Spencer, sweet Spencer, I adopt thee here :
And merely of our love we do create thee
Earl of Gloucester, and Lord Chamberlain,
Despite of times, despite of enemies.
    Y. Spen. My lord, here's a messenger from the
        barons
Desires access unto your majesty.
    Edw. Admit him near.

Enter the HERALD *from the Barons, with his coat of arms.*

    Her. Long live King Edward, England's lawful
        lord !
    Edw. So wish not they I wis that sent thee hither.
Thou com'st from Mortimer and his complices,

A ranker rout of rebels never was.
Well, say thy message.
Her. The barons up in arms, by me salute
Your highness with long life and happiness ;
And bid me say, as plainer to your grace,
That if without effusion of blood,
You will this grief have ease and remedy,
That from your princely person you remove
This Spencer, as a putrefying branch,
That deads the royal vine, whose golden leaves
Empale your princely head, your diadem,
Whose brightness such pernicious upstarts dim,
Say they ; and lovingly advise your grace,
To cherish virtue and nobility,
And have old servitors in high esteem,
And shake off smooth dissembling flatterers :
This granted, they, their honours, and their lives,
Are to your highness vowed and consecrate.
   Y. Spen. Ah, traitors ! will they still display their
      pride ?
   Edw. Away, tarry no answer, but be gone !
Rebels, will they appoint their sovereign
His sports, his pleasures, and his company ?
Yet, ere thou go, see how I do divorce
                        [*Embraces* SPENCER.
Spencer from me.—Now get thee to thy lords,
And tell them I will come to chastise them
For murthering Gaveston ; hie thee, get thee gone !
Edward with fire and sword follows at thy heels.
My lords, perceive you how these rebels swell ?
Soldiers, good hearts, defend your sovereign's right,
For now, even now, we march to make them stoop.
Away !   [*Exeunt. Alarums, excursions, a great
         fight, and a retreat.*
                (G)

SCENE III.

Enter the KING, Old SPENCER, Young SPENCER, *and the* NOBLEMEN *of the King's side.*

Edw. Why do we sound retreat? upon them, lords!
This day I shall pour vengeance with my sword
On those proud rebels that are up in arms,
And do confront and countermand their king.

    Y. Spen. I doubt it not, my lord, right will prevail.

    O. Spen. 'Tis not amiss, my liege, for either part
To breathe awhile ; our men, with sweat and dust
All choked well near, begin to faint for heat ;
And this retire refresheth horse and man.

    Y. Spen. Here come the rebels.

Enter the BARONS, MORTIMER, LANCASTER, WARWICK, PEMBROKE, *etc.*

    Y. Mor. Look, Lancaster, yonder is Edward among his flatterers.

    Lan. And there let him be
Till he pay dearly for their company.

    War. And shall, or Warwick's sword shall smite in vain.

    Edw. What, rebels, do you shrink and sound retreat?

    Y. Mor. No, Edward, no, thy flatterers faint and fly.

    Lan. They'd best betimes forsake thee, and their trains,
For they'll betray thee, traitors as they are.

    Y. Spen. Traitor on thy face, rebellious Lancaster!

    Pem. Away, base upstart, bravest thou nobles thus?

    O. Spen. A noble attempt and honourable deed,

I& it not, trow ye, to assemble aid,
And levy arms against your lawful king !
    Edw. For which ere long their heads shall satisfy,
To appease the wrath of their offended king.
    Y. Mor. Then, Edward, thou wilt fight it to the last,
And rather bathe thy sword in subjects' blood,
Than banish that pernicious company ?
    Edw. Aye, traitors, all, rather than thus be braved,
Make England's civil towns huge heaps of stones,
And ploughs to go about our palace-gates.
    War. A desperate and unnatural resolution !
Alarum !—to the fight !
St. George for England, and the barons' right.
    Edw. St. George for England, and King Edward's
    right.   [*Alarums. Exeunt.*

Re-enter EDWARD *and his followers, with the* BARONS
and KENT *captives.*

    Edw. Now, lusty lords, now, not by chance of war,
But justice of the quarrel and the cause,
Vailed is your pride ; methinks you hang the heads,
But we'll advance them, traitors : now 'tis time
To be avenged on you for all your braves,
And for the murder of my dearest friend,
To whom right well you knew our soul was knit,
Good Pierce of Gaveston, my sweet favourite.
Ah, rebels ! recreants ! you made him away.
    Kent. Brother, in regard of thee, and of thy land,
Did they remove that flatterer from thy throne.
    Edw. So, sir, you have spoke ; away, avoid our
    presence !   [*Exit* KENT.
Accursèd wretches, was't in regard of us,
When we had sent our messenger to request
He might be spared to come to speak with us,

And Pembroke undertook for his return,
That thou, proud Warwick, watched the prisoner,
Poor Pierce, and headed him 'gainst law of arms ;
For which thy head shall overlook the rest,
As much as thou in rage outwent'st the rest.
    War. Tyrant, I scorn thy threats and menaces,
It is but temporal that thou canst inflict.
    Lan. The worst is death, and better die to live
Than live in infamy under such a king.
    Edw. Away with them, my lord of Winchester !
These lusty leaders, Warwick and Lancaster,
I charge you roundly—off with both their heads ;
Away !
    War. Farewell, vain world !
    Lan. Sweet Mortimer, farewell !
    Y. Mor. England, unkind to thy nobility,
Groan for this grief, behold how thou art maimed !
    Edw. Go, take that haughty Mortimer to the
        Tower,
There see him safe bestowed ; and for the rest,
Do speedy execution on them all.
Begone !
    Y. Mor. What, Mortimer ! can ragged stony walls
Immure thy virtue that aspires to heaven ?
No, Edward, England's scourge, it may not be,
Mortimer's hope surmounts his fortune far.
                    [*The captive* BARONS *are led off.*
    Edw. Sound drums and trumpets ! March with me,
        my friends,
Edward this day hath crowned him king anew.
            [*Exeunt all except* Young SPENCER, LEVUNE,
                    and BALDOCK.
    Y. Spen. Levune, the trust that we repose in thee
Begets the quiet of King Edward's land.

Therefore begone in haste, and with advice
Bestow that treasure on the lords of France,
That, therewith all enchanted, like the guard
That suffered Jove to pass in showers of gold
To Danaë, all aid may be denied
To Isabel, the queen, that now in France
Makes friends, to cross the seas with her young son,
And step into his father's regiment.
   Levune. That's it these barons and the subtle queen
Long levelled at.
   Bal. Yea, but, Levune, thou seest,
These barons lay their heads on blocks together ;
What they intend, the hangman frustrates clean.
   Levune. Have you no doubt, my lords, I'll clap so
   close
Among the lords of France with England's gold,
That Isabel shall make her plaints in vain,
And France shall be obdurate with her tears.
   Y. Spen. Then make for France amain—Levune,
   away !
Proclaim King Edward's wars and victories.
                         [*Exeunt omnes.*

ACT THE FOURTH.

SCENE I.

Enter KENT.

   Kent. Fair blows the wind for France ; blow, gentle
   gale,
Till Edmund be arrived for England's good !
Nature, yield to my country's cause in this.
A brother ? no, a butcher of thy friends !
Proud Edward, dost thou banish me thy presence ?
But I'll to France, and cheer the wrongèd queen,

And certify what Edward's looseness is.
Unnatural king ! to slaughter noble men
And cherish flatterers !   Mortimer, I stay
Thy sweet escape ; stand gracious, gloomy night, to
    his device.

Enter Young MORTIMER, *disguised.*

   Y. Mor. Holloa ! who walketh there ?
Is't you, my lord ?
   Kent. Mortimer, 'tis I ;
But hath thy potion wrought so happily ?
   Y. Mor. It hath, my lord ; the warders all asleep,
I thank them, gave me leave to pass in peace.
But hath your grace got shipping unto France ?
   Kent. Fear it not.   [*Exeunt.*

SCENE II.

Enter the QUEEN *and her* SON.

   Queen. Ah, boy ! our friends do fail us all in
        France ;
The lords are cruel, and the king unkind ;
What shall we do ?
   Prince. Madam, return to England,
And please my father well, and then a fig
For all my uncle's friendship here in France.
I warrant you, I'll win his highness quickly ;
He loves me better than a thousand Spencers.
   Queen. Ah, boy ! thou art deceived, at least in this,
To think that we can yet be tuned together ;
No, no, we jar too far.   Unkind Valois !
Unhappy Isabel ! when France rejects,
Whither, oh ! whither dost thou bend thy steps ?

Enter Sir JOHN OF HENAULT.

Sir J. Madam, what cheer?

Queen. Ah ! good Sir John of Henault,
Never so cheerless, nor so far distrest.

Sir J. I hear, sweet lady, of the king's unkindness ;
But droop not, madam, noble minds contemn
Despair : will your grace with me to Henault,
And there stay time's advantage with your son ?
How say you, my lord, will you go with your friends,
And shake off all our fortunes equally ?

Prince. So pleaseth the queen, my mother, me it
likes :
The king of England, nor the court of France,
Shall have me from my gracious mother's side,
Till I be strong enough to break a staff ;
And then have at the proudest Spencer's head !

Sir J. Well said, my lord.

Queen. Oh, my sweet heart, how do I moan thy
wrongs,
Yet triumph in the hope of thee, my joy !
Ah, sweet Sir John ! even to the utmost verge
Of Europe, or the shore of Tanais,
We will with thee to Henault—so we will :
The marquis is a noble gentleman ;
His grace, I dare presume, will welcome me.
But who are these ?

Enter KENT *and* Young MORTIMER.

Kent. Madam, long may you live,
Much happier than your friends in England do !

Queen. Lord Edmund and Lord Mortimer alive !
Welcome to France ! the news was here, my lord
That you were dead, or very near your death.

Y. Mor. Lady, the last was truest of the twain ;
But Mortimer, reserved for better hap,
Hath shaken off the thraldom of the Tower,
And lives t' advance your standard, good my lord.
    Prince. How mean you an the king, my father,
        lives ?
No, my Lord Mortimer, not I, I trow.
    Queen. Not, son ; why not ? I would it were no
        worse.
But, gentle lords, friendless we are in France.
    Y. Mor. Monsieur le Grand, a noble friend of yours,
Told us, at our arrival, all the news ;
How hard the nobles, how unkind the king
Hath showed himself ; but, madam, right makes room
Where weapons wont: and, though so many friends
Are made away, as Warwick, Lancaster,
And others of our part and faction ;
Yet have we friends, assure your grace, in England
Would cast up caps, and clap their hands for joy,
To see us there, appointed for our foes.
    Kent. Would all were well, and Edward well re-
        claimed,
For England's honour, peace, and quietness.
    Y. Mor. But by the sword, my lord, 't must be
        deserved ;
The king will ne'er forsake his flatterers.
    Sir J. My lords of England, sith th' ungentle king
Of France refuseth to give aid of arms
To this distressèd queen his sister here,
Go you with her to Henault ; doubt ye not,
We will find comfort, money, men, and friends
Ere long, to bid the English king a base.
Now say, young prince, what think you of the match ?
    Prince. I think King Edward will outrun us all.

Queen. Nay, son, not so; and you must not dis-
courage
Your friends, that are so forward in your aid.
Kent. Sir John of Henault, pardon us, I pray;
These comforts that you give our woful queen
Bind us in kindness all at your command.
Queen. Yea, gentle brother; and the God of heaven
Prosper your happy motion, good Sir John.
Y. Mor. This noble gentleman, forward in arms,
Was born, I see, to be our anchor-hold.
Sir John of Henault, be it thy renown,
That England's queen, and nobles in distress,
Have been by thee restored and comforted.
Sir J. Madam, along, and you my lord, with me,
That England's peers may Henault's welcome see.

[*Exeunt.*

SCENE III.

Enter the KING, ARUNDEL, *the two* SPENCERS,
with others.

Edw. Thus after many threats of wrathful war,
Triumpheth England's Edward with his friends;
And triumph, Edward, with friends uncontrolled!
My lord of Gloucester, do you hear the news?
Y. Spen. What news, my lord?
Edw. Why man, they say there is great execution
Done through the realm; my lord of Arundel,
You have the note, have you not?
Arun. From the lieutenant of the Tower, my lord.
Edw. I pray let us see it. What have we there?
Read it, Spencer. [SPENCER *reads their names.*
Why so; they barked apace a month ago:
Now, on my life, they'll neither bark nor bite.

Now, sirs, the news from France ? Gloucester, I trow,
The lords of France love England's gold so well,
As Isabella gets no aid from thence.
What now remains ; have you proclaimed, my lord,
Reward for them can bring in Mortimer ?
    Y. Spen. My lord, we have ; and if he be in
        England,
He will be had ere long, I doubt it not.
    Edw. If, dost thou say ? Spencer, as true as death,
He is in England's ground ; our portmasters
Are not so careless of their king's command.

Enter a MESSENGER.

How now, what news with thee ? from whence comes
    these ?
    Mes. Letters, my lord, and tidings forth of France,
To you, my lord of Gloucester, from Levune.
    Edw. Read.

[SPENCER *reads the letter.*]

*My duty to your honour premised, etc. I have,
    ling to instructions in that behalf, dealt with the
    of France his lords, and effected, that the queen, all
    ented and discomforted, is gone. Whither, if you
    ith Sir John of Henault, brother to the marquis,
    landers : with them are gone Lord Edmund, and
    Lord Mortimer, having in their company divers of
    ur nation, and others ; and, as constant report goeth,
    they intend to give King Edward battle in England, sooner
    than he can look for them : this is all the news of import.*
        " *Your honour's in all service,* LEVUNE."

    Edw. Ah villains ! hath that Mortimer escaped ?
With him is Edmund gone associate ?

And will Sir John of Henault lead the round?
Welcome, a God's name, madam, and your son ;
England shall welcome you and all your rout.
Gallop apace, bright Phœbus, through the sky,
And dusty night, in rusty iron car,
Between you both shorten the time, I pray,
That I may see that most desirèd day,
When we may meet these traitors in the field.
Ah, nothing grieves me, but my little boy
Is thus misled to countenance their ills.
Come, friends, to Bristow, there to make us strong ;
And, winds, as equal be to bring them in,
As you injurious were to bear them forth !   [*Exeunt.*

SCENE IV.

Enter the QUEEN, *her* SON, KENT, MORTIMER, *and*
SIR JOHN.

Queen. Now, lords, our loving friends and country-
men,
Welcome to England all ; with prosperous winds,
Our kindest friends in Belgia have we left,
To cope with friends at home ; a heavy case
When force to force is knit, and sword and glaive
In civil broils make kin and countrymen
Slaughter themselves in others, and their sides
With their own weapons gore !   But what's the help ?
Misgoverned kings are cause of all this wreck ;
And, Edward, thou art one among them all,
Whose looseness hath betrayed thy land to spoil,
Who made the channel overflow with blood
Of thine own people ; patron shouldst thou be,
But thou——

Y. Mor. Nay, madam, if you be a warrior,
Ye must not grow so passionate in speeches.
Lords, sith we are, by sufferance of heaven,
Arrived, and armèd in this prince's right,
Here for our country's cause swear we to him
All homage, fealty, and forwardness ;
And for the open wrongs and injuries
Edward hath done to us, his queen, and land,
We come in arms to wreak it with the sword ;
That England's queen in peace may repossess
Her dignities and honours : and withal
We may remove those flatterers from the king,
That havoc England's wealth and treasury.
　　Sir J. Sound trumpets, my lord, and forward let us
　　　march.
Edward will think we come to flatter him.
　　Kent. I would he never had been flattered more !
　　　　　　　　　　　　　　　　　　　　　　[*Exeunt.*

SCENE V.

Enter the KING, BALDOCK, *and* Young SPENCER,
　　　　flying about the stage.

　　Y. Spen. Fly, fly, my lord ! the queen is over-
　　　strong ;
Her friends do multiply, and yours do fail.
Shape we our course to Ireland, there to breathe.
　　Edw. What ! was I born to fly and run away,
And leave the Mortimers conquerors behind ?
Give me my horse, let's reinforce our troops :
And in this bed of honour die with fame.
　　Bald. O no, my lord, this princely resolution
Fits not the time ; away, we are pursued.　　[*Exeunt.*

Enter KENT *alone, with his sword and target.*

Kent. This way he fled, but I am come too late.
Edward, alas ! my heart relents for thee.
Proud traitor, Mortimer, why dost thou chase
Thy lawful king, thy sovereign, with thy sword ?
Vile wretch ! and why hast thou, of all unkind,
Borne arms against thy brother and thy king ?
Rain showers of vengeance on thy cursèd head,
Thou God, to whom in justice it belcngs
To punish this unnatural revolt !
Edward, this Mortimer aims at thy life :
O fly him then ! but Edmund, calm this rage,
Dissemble, or thou diest ; for Mortimer
And Isabel do kiss, while they conspire :
And yet she bears a face of love forsooth.
Fie on that love that hatcheth death and hate !
Edmund, away ; Bristow to Longshanks' blood
Is false ; be not found single for suspect :
Proud Mortimer pries near into thy walks.

Enter the QUEEN, MORTIMER, *the* Young PRINCE, *and*
SIR JOHN OF HENAULT.

Queen. Successful battle gives the God of kings
To them that fight in right, and fear his wrath.
Since then successfully we have prevailed,
Thanked be heaven's great architect, and you.
Ere farther we proceed, my noble lords,
We here create our well-beloved son,
Of love and care unto his royal person,
Lord Warden of the realm, and sith the fates
Have made his father so infortunate,
Deal you, my lords, in this, my loving lords,
As to your wisdoms fittest seems in all.

Kent. Madam, without offence, if I may ask,
How will you deal with Edward in his fall?
   Prince. Tell me, good uncle, what Edward do you
     mean?
   Kent. Nephew, your father; I dare not call him
     king.
   Mor. My lord of Kent, what needs these questions?
'Tis not in her controlment, nor in ours,
But as the realm and parliament shall please,
So shall your brother be disposèd of.
I like not this relenting mood in Edmund.
Madam, 'tis good to look to him betimes.
                 [*Aside to the* QUEEN.
   Queen. My lord, the Mayor of Bristow knows our
     mind.
   Y. Mor. Yea, madam, and they 'scape not easily
That fled the field.
   Queen. Baldock is with the king.
A goodly chancellor is he not, my lord?
   Sir J. So are the Spencers, the father and the
     son.
   Kent. This Edward is the ruin of the realm.

Enter RICE AP HOWELL, *and the* MAYOR OF BRISTOW,
   with Old SPENCER *prisoner.*

   Rice. God save queen Isabel, and her princely
     son!
Madam, the mayor and citizens of Bristow,
In sign of love and duty to this presence,
Present by me this traitor to the state,
Spencer, the father to that wanton Spencer,
That, like the lawless Catiline of Rome,
Revelled in England's wealth and treasury.

Queen. We thank you all.

Y. Mor. Your loving care in this
Deserveth princely favours and rewards.
But where's the king and the other Spencer fled?

Rice. Spencer the son, created Earl of Gloucester,
Is with that smooth-tongued scholar Baldock gone,
And shipped but late for Ireland with the king.

Y. Mor. Some whirlwind fetch them back or sink
    them all!   *[Aside.*
They shall be started thence, I doubt it not.

Prince. Shall I not see the king my father yet?

Kent. Unhappy Edward, chased from England's
    bounds.

Sir J. Madam, what resteth, why stand you in a
    muse?

Queen. I rue my lord's ill-fortune; but alas!
Care of my country called me to this war.

Y. Mor. Madam, have done with care and sad
    complaint;
Your king hath wronged your country and himself,
And we must seek to right it as we may.
Meanwhile, have hence this rebel to the block.

O. Spen. Rebel is he that fights against the
    prince;
So fought not they that fought in Edward's right.

Y. Mor. Take him away, he prates; you, Rice ap
    Howell,
Shall do good service to her majesty,
Being of countenance in your country here,
To follow these rebellious runagates.
We in meanwhile, madam, must take advice,
How Baldock, Spencer, and their complices,
May in their fall be followed to their end.
                         [Exeunt omnes.

SCENE VI.

Enter the ABBOT, MONKS, EDWARD, SPENCER,
and BALDOCK.

Abbot. Have you no doubt, my lord ; have you no
    fear ;
As silent and as careful we will be,
To keep your royal person safe with us,
Free from suspect, and fell invasion
Of such as have your majesty in chase,
Yourself, and those your chosen company,
As danger of this stormy time requires.
    Edw. Father, thy face should harbour no deceit.
O ! hadst thou ever been a king, thy heart,
Pierced deeply with a sense of my distress,
Could not but take compassion of my state,
Stately and proud, in riches and in train,
Whilom I was, powerful, and full of pomp :
But what is he whom rule and empery
Have not in life or death made miserable ?
Come Spencer, Baldock come, sit down by me ;
Make trial now of thy philosophy,
That in our famous nurseries of arts
Thou suck'dst from Plato and from Aristotle,
Father, this life contemplative is heaven.
O that I might this life in quiet lead !
But we, alas ! are chased ; and you, my friends,
Your lives and my dishonour they pursue.
Yet, gentle monks, for treasure, gold, nor fee,
Do you betray us and our company.
    Monk. Your grace may sit secure, if none but we
Do wot of your abode.
    Y. Spen. Not one alive, but shrewdly I suspect
A gloomy fellow in a mead below.

He gave a long look after us, my lord,
And all the land I know is up in arms,
Arms that pursue our lives with deadly hate.
Bald. We were embarked for Ireland, wretched wo !
With awkward winds and sore tempests driven
To fall on shore, and here to pine in fear
Of Mortimer and his confederates.
Edw. Mortimer ! who talks of Mortimer ?
Who wounds me with the name of Mortimer ?
That bloody man ! Good father, on thy lap
Lay I this head, laden with mickle care.
O might I never ope these eyes again !
Never again lift up this drooping head !
O never more lift up this dying heart !
Y. Spen. Look up, my lord.—Baldock, this drowsiness
Betides no good ; even here we are betrayed.

Enter, with Welsh hooks, RICE AP HOWELL, *a* MOWER,
and the EARL OF LEICESTER.

Mow. Upon my life, these be the men ye seek.
Rice. Fellow, enough. My lord, I pray be short,
A fair commission warrants what we do.
Leices. The queen's commission, urged by Mortimer :
What cannot gallant Mortimer with the queen ?
Alas ! see where he sits, and hopes unseen
To escape their hands that seek to reave his life.
Too true it is, *quem dies vidit veniens superbum,
Hunc dies vidit fugiens jacentem.*
But, Leicester, leave to grow so passionate.
Spencer and Baldock, by no other names,
I do arrest you of high treason here.
Stand not on titles, but obey the arrest,
(H)

'Tis in the name of Isabel the queen.
My lord, why droop you thus?
   Edw. O day, the last of all my bliss on earth!
Centre of all misfortune! O my stars,
Why do you lour unkindly on a king?
Comes Leicester then in Isabella's name,
To take my life, my company from me?
Here, man, rip up this panting breast of mine,
And take my heart in rescue of my friends.
   Rice. Away with them!
   Y. Spen. It may become thee yet,
To let us take our farewell of his grace.
   Abbot. My heart with pity yearns to see this
      sight,
A king to bear these words and proud commands.
   Edw. Spencer, sweet Spencer, thus then must we
      part?
   Y. Spen. We must, my lord, so will the angry
   heavens.
   Edw. Nay, so will hell and cruel Mortimer;
The gentle heavens have not to do in this.
   Bald. My lord, it is in vain to grieve or storm
Here humbly of your grace we take our leaves;
Our lots are cast, I fear me, so is thine.
   Edw. In heaven we may, in earth ne'er shall we
      meet:
And, Leicester, say, what shall become of us?
   Leices. Your majesty must go to Killingworth
   Edw. Must! it is somewhat hard, when kings must
      go.
   Leices. Here is a litter ready for your grace,
That waits your pleasure, and the day grows old.
   Rice. As good be gone, as stay and be benighted.
   Edw. A litter hast thou? lay me on a hearse,

And to the gates of hell convey me hence ;
Let Pluto's bells ring out my fatal knell,
And hags howl for my death at Charon's shore,
For friend hath [hapless] Edward none, but these ;
And these must die under a tyrant's sword.
  Rice. My lord, be going ; care not for these,
For we shall see them shorter by the heads.
  Edw. Well, that shall be, shall be : part we must !
Sweet Spencer, gentle Baldock, part me must !
Hence feignèd weeds ! unfeignèd are my woes:
                              [*Casts off his disguise.*
Father, farewell ! Leicester, thou stay'st for me,
And go I must.   Life, farewell, with my friends.
                    [*Exeunt* EDWARD *and* LEICESTER.
  Y. Spen. Oh, is he gone ! is noble Edward gone !
Parted from hence ? never to see us more ?
Rent, sphere of heaven ! and, fire, forsake thy orb !
Earth, melt to air ! gone is my sovereign,
Gone, gone, alas ! never to make return.
  Bald. Spencer, I see our souls are fleeting hence ;
We are deprived the sunshine of our life :
Make for a new life, man ; throw up thy eyes,
And heart and hands to heaven's immortal throne ;
Pay nature's debt with cheerful countenance ;
Reduce we all our lessons unto this,
To die, sweet Spencer, therefore live we all ;
Spencer, all live to die, and rise to fall.
  Rice. Come, come, keep these preachments till you
    come to the place appointed.
You, and such as you are, have made wise work in
    England ; will your lordships away ?
  Mow. Your lordship I trust will remember me ?
  Rice. Remember thee, fellow ! what else ? Follow
    me to the town.   [*Exeunt.*

ACT THE FIFTH.

Scene I.

Enter the King, Leicester, *the* Bishop of
Winchester, *and* Trussel.

Leices. Be patient, good my lord, cease to lament ;
Imagine Killingworth Castle were your court,
And that you lay for pleasure here a space,
Not of compulsion or necessity.
　　Edw. Leicester, if gentle words might comfort me,
Thy speeches long ago had eased my sorrows,
For kind and loving hast thou always been.
The griefs of private men are soon allay'd ;
But not of kings.　The forest deer, being struck,
Runs to an herb that closeth up the wounds :
But when the imperial lion's flesh is gored,
He rends and tears it with his wrathful paw,
And highly scorning that the lowly earth
Should drink his blood, mounts up to the air :
And so it fares with me, whose dauntless mind
The ambitious Mortimer would seek to curb,
And that unnatural queen, false Isabel,
That thus hath pent and mew'd me in a prison ;
For such outrageous passions cloy my soul,
As with the wings of rancour and disdain
Full often am I soaring up to heaven,
To plain me to the gods against them both.
But when I call to mind I am a king,
Methinks I should revenge me of my wrongs,
That Mortimer and Isabel have done.
But what are kings, when regiment is gone,
But perfect shadows in a sunshine day ?
My nobles rule ; I bear the name of king ;

I wear the crown ; but am controlled by them,
By Mortimer, and my unconstant queen,
Who spots my nuptial bed with infamy ;
Whilst I am lodged within this cave of care,
Where sorrow at my elbow still attends,
To company my heart with sad laments,
That bleeds within me for this strange exchange.
But tell me, must I now resign my crown,
To make usurping Mortimer a king ?
   Winch. Your grace mistakes ; it is for England's
    good,
And princely Edward's right, we crave the crown.
   Edw. No, 'tis for Mortimer, not Edward's head ;
For he's a lamb, encompassed by wolves,
Which in a moment will abridge his life.
But, if proud Mortimer do wear this crown,
Heaven turn it to a blaze of quenchless fire
Or, like the snaky wreath of Tisiphon,
Engirt the temples of his hateful head !
So shall not England's vine be perished,
But Edward's name survive, though Edward dies.
   Leices. My lord, why waste you thus the time
    away ?
They stay your answer : will you yield your crown ?
   Edw. Ah, Leicester, weigh how hardly I can brook
To lose my crown and kingdom without cause ;
To give ambitious Mortimer my right,
That, like a mountain, overwhelms my bliss ;
In which extreme my mind here murthered is !
But that the heavens appoint I must obey.—
Here, take my crown ; the life of Edward too :
                [*Taking off the crown.*
Two kings in England cannot reign at once.
But stay awhile : let me be king till night,

That I may gaze upon this glittering crown ;
So shall my eyes receive their last content,
My head, the latest honour due to it,
And jointly both yield up their wishèd right.
Continue ever, thou celestial sun ;
Let never silent night possess this clime ;
Stand still, you watches of the element ;
All times and seasons, rest you at a stay,
That Edward may be still fair England's king !
But day's bright beam doth vanish fast away,
And needs I must resign my wishèd crown.
Inhuman creatures, nursed with tiger's milk,
Why gape you for your sovereign's overthrow ?
My diadem, I mean, and guiltless life.
See, monsters, see ! I'll wear my crown again.
                          [*He puts on the crown.*
What, fear you not the fury of your king ?—
But, hapless Edward, thou art fondly led ;
They pass not for thy frowns as late they did,
But seek to make a new-elected king ;
Which fills my mind with strange despairing thoughts,
Which thoughts are martyrèd with endless torments ;
And in this torment comfort find I none,
But that I feel the crown upon my head ;
And therefore let me wear it yet awhile.   [news ;
    Trus. My lord, the parliament must have present
And therefore say, will you resign or no ?
                          [*The* KING *rageth.*
    Edw. I'll not resign, not whilst I live !
Traitors, be gone ! join you with Mortimer !
Elect, conspire, install, do what you will :
Their blood and yours shall seal these treacheries.
    Winch. This answer we'll return ; and so, farewell.
                          [*Going with* TRUSSEL.

Leices. Call them again, my lord, and speak them
 fair ;
For, if they go, the prince shall lose his right.
Edw. Call thou them back ; I have no power to
 speak.
Leices. My lord, the king is willing to resign.
Winch. If he be not, let him choose.
Edw. O, would I might ! but heavens and earth
 conspire
To make me miserable. Here, receive my crown.
Receive it ? No, these innocent hands of mine
Shall not be guilty of so foul a crime :
He of you all that most desires my blood,
And will be called the muitherer of a king,
Take it. What, are you mov'd ? pity you me ?
Then send for unrelenting Mortimer,
And Isabel, whose eyes being turn'd to steel
Will sooner sparkle fire than shed a tear.
Yet stay ; for, rather than I'll look on them,
Here, here ! [*Gives the crown.*]—Now, sweet God of
 heaven,
Make me despise this transitory pomp,
And sit for ever enthronized in heaven !
Come, death, and with thy fingers close my eyes,
Or, if I live, let me forget myself !
 Winch. My lord.
 Edw. Call me not lord ; away—out of my sight ;
Ah, pardon me : grief makes me lunatic !
Let not that Mortimer protect my son ;
More safety is there in a tiger's jaws
Than his embracements—bear this to the queen,
Wet with my tears, and dried again with sighs ;
 [*Gives a handkerchief.*
If with the sight thereof she be not moved,

Return it back, and dip it in my blood.
Commend me to my son, and bid him rule
Better than I.   Yet how have I transgrest,
Unless it be with too much clemency ?
 Trus. And thus most humbly do we take our leave.
     [*Exeunt* BISHOP *and* Attendants.
 Edw. Farewell ; I know the next news that they
  bring
Will be my death : and welcome shall it be ;
To wretched men, death is felicity.

 Enter BERKELEY, *who gives a paper to* LEICESTER.

 Leices. Another post ! what news brings he ?
 Edw. Such news as I expect—come, Berkeley, come,
And tell thy message to my naked breast.
 Berk. My lord, think not a thought so villainous
Can harbour in a man of noble birth.
To do your highness service and devoir,
And save you from your foes, Berkeley would die.
 Leices. My lord, the council of the queen commands
That I resign my charge.
 Edw. And who must keep me now ?   Must you, my
  lord ?
 Berk. Aye, my most gracious lord—so 'tis decreed.
 Edw. [*taking the paper*].   By Mortimer, whose
  name is written here !
Well may I rent his name that rends my heart.
        [*Tears it.*
This poor revenge hath something eased my mind.
So may his limbs be torn, as is this paper !
Hear me, immortal Jove, and grant it too !
 Berk. Your grace must hence with me to Berkeley
  straight.

Edw. Whither you will, all places are alike,
And every earth is fit for burial.
Leices. Favour him, my lord, as much as lieth in
you.
Berk. Even so betide my soul as I use him.
Edw. Mine enemy hath pitied my estate,
And that's the cause that I am now removed.
Berk. And thinks your grace that Berkeley will be
cruel ?
Edw. I know not ; but of this am I assured,
That death ends all, and I can die but once.
Leicester, farewell !
Leices. Not yet, my lord ; I'll bear you on your way.
[*Exeunt omnes.*

SCENE II.

Enter MORTIMER *and* QUEEN ISABEL.

Y. Mor. Fair Isabel, now have we our desire,
The proud corrupters of the light-brained king
Have done their homage to the lofty gallows,
And he himself lies in captivity.
Be ruled by me, and we will rule the realm.
In any case take heed of childish fear,
For now we hold an old wolf by the ears,
That if he slip will seize upon us both,
And gripe the sorer, being gript himself.
Think therefore, madam, it imports us much
To erect your son with all the speed we may,
And that I be protector over him ;
For our behoof, 'twill bear the greater sway
Whenas a king's name shall be under writ.
Queen. Sweet Mortimer, the life of Isabel,
Be thou persuaded that I love thee well,

And therefore, so the prince my son be safe,
Whom I esteem as dear as these mine eyes,
Conclude against his father what thou wilt,
And I myself will willingly subscribe.

    Y. Mor. First would I hear news [that] he were
        deposed,
And then let me alone to handle him.

Enter MESSENGER.

Letters! from whence?
    Mess. From Killingworth, my lord.
    Queen. How fares my lord the king?
    Mess. In health, madam, but full of pensiveness.
    Queen. Alas, poor soul, would I could ease his grief!

Enter WINCHESTER *with the Crown.*

Thanks, gentle Winchester, [*To the Messenger.*] Sirrah,
    be gone.   [*Exit Messenger.*
    Winch. The king hath willingly resigned his crown.
    Queen. Oh happy news! send for the prince, my
        son.
    Winch. Further, ere this was sealed, Lord Berkeley
        came,
So that he now is gone from Killingworth;
And we have heard that Edmund laid a plot
To set his brother free; no more but so.
The lord of Berkeley is as pitiful
As Leicester that had charge of him before.
    Queen. Then let some other be his guardian.
    Y. Mor. Let me alone, here is the privy seal.
Who's there?—call hither Gurney and Matrevis.
To dash the heavy-headed Edmund's drift,
Berkeley shall be discharged, the king removed,
And none but we shall know where he lieth.

Queen. But, Mortimer, as long as he survives,
What safety rests for us, or for my son ?
Y. Mor. Speak, shall he presently be despatched
and die.
Queen. I would he were, so't were not by my means.

Enter MATREVIS *and* GURNEY.

Y. Mor. Enough ; Matrevis, write a letter presently
Unto the lord of Berkeley from ourself
That he resign the king to thee and Gurney ;
And when 'tis done, we will subscribe our name.
Mat. It shall be done, my lord.
Y. Mor. Gurney.
Gur. My lord.
Y. Mor. As thou intend'st to rise by Mortimer,
Who now makes Fortune's wheel turn as he please,
Seek all the means thou can to make him droop,
And neither give him kind word nor good look.
Gur. I warrant you, my lord.
Y. Mor. And this above the rest, because we hear
That Edmund casts to work his liberty,
Remove him still from place to place by night,
Till at the last he come to Killingworth,
And then from thence to Berkeley back again.
And by the way, to make him fret the more,
Speak curstly to him ; and in any case
Let no man comfort him if he chance to weep,
But amplify his grief with bitter words.
Mat. Fear not, my lord, we'll do as you command.
Y. Mor. So now away ; post thitherwards amain.
Queen. Whither goes this letter ? to my lord the
king !
Commend me humbly to his majesty,
And tell him that I labour all in vain

To ease his grief, and work his liberty ;
And bear him this as witness of my love.

[*Gives a ring.*

Mat. I will, madam.

[*Exeunt all but* ISABEL *and* MORTIMER.

Enter the YOUNG PRINCE, *and the* EARL OF KENT
talking with him.

Y. Mor. Finely dissembled ?   Do so still, sweet
queen.
Here comes the young prince, with the Earl of Kent.
Queen. Something he whispers in his childish ears.
Y. Mor. If he have such access unto the prince,
Our plots and stratagems will soon be dashed.
Queen. Use Edmund friendly, as if all were well.
Y. Mor. How fares my honourable lord of Kent ?
Kent. In health, sweet Mortimer : how fares your
grace ?
Queen. Well, if my lord your brother were enlarged.
Kent. I hear of late he hath deposed himself.
Queen. The more my grief.
Y. Mor. And mine.
Kent. Ah, they do dissemble !   [*Aside.*
Queen. Sweet son, come hither, I must talk with
thee.
Y. Mor. You being his uncle, and the next of
blood,
Do look to be protector o'er the prince.
Kent. Not I, my lord ; who should protect the son,
But she that gave him life ; I mean the queen ?
Prince. Mother, persuade me not to wear the crown :
Let him be king—I am too young to reign.
Queen. But be content, seeing 't is his highness'
pleasures.

Prince. Let me but see him first, and then I will.

Kent. Ay, do, sweet nephew.

Queen. Brother, you know it is impossible.

Prince. Why, is he dead ?

Queen. No, God forbid.

Kent. I would those words proceeded from your heart.

Y. Mor. Inconstant Edmund, dost thou favour him, That wast a cause of his imprisonment ?

Kent. The more cause have I now to make amends.

Y. Mor. I tell thee, 'tis not meet that one so false Should come about the person of a prince.
My lord, he hath betrayed the king his brother, And therefore trust him not.

Prince. But he repents, and sorrows for it now.

Queen. Come, son, and go with this gentle lord and me.

Prince. With you I will, but not with Mortimer.

Y. Mor. Why, youngling, 'sdain'st thou so of Mortimer ?
Then I will carry thee by force away.

Prince. Help, uncle Kent, Mortimer will wrong me.

Queen. Brother Edmund, strive not ; we are his friends ;
Isabel is nearer than the Earl of Kent.

Kent. Sister, Edward is my charge, redeem him.

Queen. Edward is my son, and I will keep him.

Kent. Mortimer shall know that he hath wronged me !—
Hence will I haste to Killingworth castle,
And rescue aged Edward from his foes,
To be revenged on Mortimer and thee.

              [*Aside. Exeunt omnes*

Scene III.

Enter Matrevis *and* Gurney, *with the* King.

Mat. My lord, be not pensive, we are your friends;
Men are ordained to live in misery,
Therefore come—dalliance dangereth our lives.
Edw. Friends, whither must unhappy Edward go?
Will hateful Mortimer appoint no rest?
Must I be vexèd like the nightly bird,
Whose sight is loathsome to all wingèd fowls?
When will the fury of his mind assuage!
When will his heart be satisfied with blood?
If mine will serve, unbowel straight this breast,
And give my heart to Isabel and him;
It is the chiefest mark they level at.
Gur. Not so, my liege, the queen hath given this
        charge
[Only] to keep your grace in safety:
Your passions make your dolours to increase.
Edw. This usage makes my misery increase.
But can my air of life continue long
When all my senses are annoyed with stench?
Within a dungeon England's king is kept,
Where I am starved for want of sustenance.
My daily diet is heart-breaking sobs,
That almost rent the closet of my heart;
Thus lives old Edward not relieved by any,
And so must die, though pitièd by many.
Oh, water, gentle friends, to cool my thirst,
And clear my body from foul excrements!
Mat. Here's channel water, as our charge is given;
Sit down, for we'll be barbers to your grace.
Edw. Traitors, away! what, will you murder me,
Or choke your sovereign with puddle water?

Gur. No, but wash your face, and shave away your
 beard,
Lest you be known, and so be rescued.
Mat. Why strive you thus ? your labour is in vain !
Edw. The wren may strive against the lion's strength,
But all in vain : so vainly do I strive
To seek for mercy at a tyrant's hand.
 [*They wash him with puddle water, and shave
 his beard away.*
Immortal powers ! that know the painful cares
That wait upon my poor distressèd soul !
O level your looks upon these daring men,
That wrong their liege and sovereign, England's king.
O Gaveston, 'tis for thee that I am wronged,
For me, both thou and both the Spencers died !
And for your sakes a thousand wrongs I'll take.
The Spencers' ghosts, wherever they remain,
Wish well to mine ; then tush, for them I'll die.
 Mat. 'Twixt theirs and yours shall be no enmity.
Come, come away ; now put the torches out,
We'll enter in by darkness to Killingworth.

Enter KENT.

Gur. How now, who comes there ?
Mat. Guard the king sure : it is the Earl of Kent.
Edw. O, gentle brother, help to rescue me !
Mat. Keep them asunder ; thrust in the king.
Kent. Soldiers, let me but talk to him one word.
Gur. Lay hands upon the earl for his assault.
Kent. Lay down your weapons, traitors ; yield the
 king.
Mat. Edmund, yield thou thyself, or thou shalt die.
Kent. Base villains, wherefore do you gripe me
 thus !

Gur. Bind him, and so convey him to the court.

Kent. Where is the court but here? here is the king,

And I will visit him ; why stay you me?

Mat. The court is where Lord Mortimer remains ;

Thither shall your honour go ; and so farewell.

> [*Exeunt* MATREVIS *and* GURNEY, *with the* KING.
> KENT *and the* Soldiers *remain.*

Kent. O miserable is that commonweal,

Where lords keep courts, and kings are locked in prison !

Sol. Wherefore stay we? on, sirs, to the court.

Kent. Aye, lead me whither you will, even to my death,

Seeing that my brother cannot be released.

> [*Exeunt omnes.*

SCENE IV.

Enter Young MORTIMER.

Y. Mor. The king must die, or Mortimer goes down.

The commons now begin to pity him.

Yet he that is the cause of Edward's death,

Is sure to pay for it when his son's of age ;

And therefore will I do it cunningly.

This letter, written by a friend of ours,

Contains his death, yet bids them save his life. [*Reads.*

Edwardum occidere nolite timere bonum est

Fear not to kill the king 'tis good he die.

But read it thus, and that's another sense :

Edwardum occidere nolite timere bonum est

Kill not the king 'tis good to fear the worst.

Unpointed as it is, thus shall it go,

That, being dead, if it chance to be found,
Matrevis and the rest may bear the blame,
And we be quit that caused it to be done.
Within this room is locked the messenger
That shall convey it, and perform the rest :
And by a secret token that he bears,
Shall he be murdered when the deed is done.
Lightborn, come forth ;

Enter LIGHTBORN.

Art thou so resolute as thou wast ?
  Light. What else, my lord ? and far more resolute.
  Y. Mor. And hast thou cast how to accomplish it ?
  Light. Ay, ay; and none shall know which way he
    died.
  Y. Mor. But at his looks, Lightborn, thou wilt
    relent.
  Light. Relent ! ha, ha ! I use much to relent.
  Y. Mor. Well, do it bravely, and be secret.
  Light. You shall not need to give instructions :
'Tis not the first time I have killed a man ;
I learned in Naples how to poison flowers ;
To strangle with a lawn thrust down the throat ;
To pierce the windpipe with a needle's point ;
Or, whilst one is asleep, to take a quill,
And blow a little powder in his ears ;
Or open his mouth, and pour quicksilver down.
But yet I have a braver way than these.
  Y. Mor. What's that ?
  Light. Nay, you shall pardon me ; none shall know
    my tricks.
  Y. Mor. I care not how it is, so it be not spied.
Deliver this to Gurney and Matrevis :
                        [*Gives letter.*

(1)

At every ten-mile end thou hast a horse :
Take this [*Gives money*] : away, and never see me more !
  Light. No ?
  Y. Mor. No ; unless thou bring me news of Edward's
    death.
  Light. That will I quickly do.   Farewell, my lord.
                                                                Exit.

  Y. Mor. The prince I rule, the queen do I command,
And with a lowly congé to the ground,
The proudest lords salute me as I pass :
I seal, I cancel, I do what I will ;
Feared am I more than loved—let me be feared ;
And when I frown, make all the court look pale.
I view the prince with Aristarchus' eyes,
Whose looks were as a breeching to a boy.
They thrust upon me the protectorship,
And sue to me for that that I desire.
While at the council-table, grave enough,
And not unlike a bashful puritan,
First I complain of imbecility,
Saying it is *onus quam gravissimum ;*
Till being interrupted by my friends,
Sus epi that *provinciam* as they term it ;
And to conclude, I am Protector now.
Now is all sure, the queen and Mortimer
Shall rule the realm, the king ; and none rule us.
Mine enemies will I plague, my friends advance ;
And what I list command who dare control ?
Major sum quàm cui possit fortuna nocere.
And that this be the coronation-day,
It pleaseth me, and Isabel the queen.
                                                [*Trumpets within.*
The trumpets sound, I must go take my place.

Enter the Young KING, ARCHBISHOP, CHAMPION,
NOBLES, QUEEN.

Archbish. Long live King Edward, by the grace
of God,
King of England, and Lord of Ireland !
Cham. If any Christian, Heathen, Turk, or Jew,
Dare but affirm that Edward's not true king,
And will avouch his saying with the sword,
I am the champion that will combat him.
Y. Mor. None comes, sound trumpets.
King. Champion, here's to thee.　　　[*Gives a purse.*
Queen. Lord Mortimer, now take him to your
charge.

Enter Soldiers *with the* EARL OF KENT, *prisoner.*

Y. Mor. What traitor have we there with blades
and bills?
Sol. Edmund, the Earl of Kent.
King. What hath he done?
Sol. He would have taken the king away perforce,
As we were bringing him to Killingworth.
Y. Mor. Did you attempt his rescue, Edmund?
speak.
Kent. Mortimer, I did ; he is our king,
And thou compell'st this prince to wear the crown.
Y. Mor. Strike off his head, he shall have martial law.
Kent. Strike off my head ! base traitor, I defy thee.
King. My lord, he is my uncle, and shall live.
Y. Mor. My lord, he is your enemy, and shall die.
Kent. Stay, villains !
King. Sweet mother, if I cannot pardon him,
Entreat my Lord Protector for his life.
Queen. Son, be content ; I dare not speak a word.

King. Nor I, and yet methinks I should command ;
But, seeing I cannot, I'll entreat for him—
My lord, if you will let my uncle live,
I will requite it when I come to age.
    Y. Mor. 'Tis for your highness' good, and for the
        realm's.
How often shall I bid you bear him hence ?
    Kent. Art thou king ? must I die at thy command ?
    Y. Mor. At our command ! once more, away with
        him.
    Kent. Let me but stay and speak ; I will not go.
Either my brother or his son is king,
And none of both them thirst for Edmund's blood.
And therefore, soldiers, whither will you hale me ?
    [*They hale* KENT *away and carry him to be beheaded.*
    King. What safety may I look for at his hands,
If that my uncle shall be murdered thus ?
    Queen. Fear not, sweet boy, I'll guard thee from thy
        foes ;
Had Edmund lived, he would have sought thy death.
Come, son, we'll ride a-hunting in the park.
    King. And shall my uncle Edmund ride with us ?
    Queen. He is a traitor, think not on him ; come.
                            [*Exeunt omnes.*

SCENE V.

Enter MATREVIS *and* GURNEY.

Mat. Gurney, I wonder the king dies not,
Being in a vault up to the knees in water,
To which the channels of the castle run,
From whence a damp continually ariseth,
That were enough to poison any man,
Much more a king, brought up so tenderly.

Gur. And so do I, Matrevis : yesternight
I opened but the door to throw him meat,
And I was almost stifled with the savour.
Mat. He hath a body able to endure
More than we can inflict : and therefore now
Let us assail his mind another while.
Gur. Send for him out thence, and I will anger him.
Mat. But stay ; who's this ?

Enter LIGHTBORN.

Light. My Lord Protector greets you. [*Gives letter.*
Gur. What's here ? I know not how to construe it.
Mat. Gurney, it was left unpointed for the nonce ;
Edwardum occidere nolite timere,
That's his meaning.
Light. Know ye this token ? I must have the king.
[*Gives token.*
Mat. Ay, stay a while ; thou shalt have answer
straight.
This villain's sent to make away the king.
Gur. I thought as much.
Mat. And, when the murder's done,
See how he must be handled for his labour—
Percat iste! Let him have the king ;
What else ?—Here is the keys, this is the lake :
Do as you are commanded by my lord.
Light. I know what I must do. Get you away :
Yet be not far off ; I shall need your help :
See that in the next room I have a fire,
And get me a spit, and let it be red hot.
Mat. Very well.
Gur. Need you anything besides ?
Light. A table and a feather-bed.
Gur. That's all ?

Light. Ay, ay : so, when I call you, bring it in.
Mat. Fear not thou that.
Gur. Here's a light ; go into the dungeon.

> [*Gives light to* LIGHTBORN, *and then
> exit with* MATREVIS.

Light. So, now
Must I about this gear : ne'er was there any
So finely handled as this king shall be.
Foh, here's a place indeed, with all my heart !
Edw. Who's there ? what light is that ? where-
fore com'st thou ?
Light. To comfort you, and bring you joyful news.
Edw. Small comfort finds poor Edward in thy
looks :
Villain, I know thou com'st to murder me.
Light. To murder you, my most gracious lord !
Far is it from my heart to do you harm.
The queen sent me to see how you were used,
For she relents at this your misery :
And what eyes can refrain from shedding tears,
To see a king in this most piteous state ?
Edw. Weep'st thou already ? list a while to me,
And then thy heart, were it as Gurney's is,
Or as Matrevis', hewn from the Caucasus,
Yet will it melt ere I have done my tale.
This dungeon where they keep me is the sink
Wherein the filth of all the castle falls.
Light. O villains !
Edw. And there, in mire and puddle, have I stood
This ten days' space ; and, lest that I should sleep,
One plays continually upon a drum.
They give me bread and water, being a king ;
So that, for want of sleep and sustenance,
My mind's distemper'd, and my body's numb'd,

And whether I have limbs or no I know not.
O, would my blood dropped out from every vein,
As doth this water from my tatter'd robes !
Tell Isabel the queen, I look'd not thus,
When for her sake I ran at tilt in France,
And there unhorsed the Duke of Cleremont.

    Light. O, speak no more, my lord ! this breaks my
heart.
Lie on this bed, and rest yourself a while.

    Edw. These looks of thine can harbour nought
but death ;
I see my tragedy written in thy brows.
Yet stay a while ; forbear thy bloody hand,
And let me see the stroke before it comes,
That even then when I shall lose my life,
My mind may be more steadfast on my God.

    Light. What means your highness to mistrust me
thus ?

    Edw. What mean'st thou to dissemble with me
thus ?

    Light. These hands were never stain'd with innocent
blood,
Nor shall they now be tainted with a king's.

    Edw. Forgive my thought for having such a
thought.
One jewel have I left ; receive thou this :

                              [Giving jewel.
Still fear I, and I know not what's the cause,
But every joint shakes as I give it thee.
O, if thou harbour'st murder in thy heart,
Let this gift change thy mind, and save thy soul !
Know that I am a king : O, at that name
I feel a hell of grief ! where is my crown ?
Gone, gone ! and do I remain alive ?

Light. You're overwatch'd, my lord : lie down and
rest.

Edw. But that grief keeps me waking, I should
sleep ;
For not these ten days have these eye-lids closed.
Now, as I speak, they fall ; and yet with fear
Open again.   O, wherefore sitt'st thou here ?

Light. If you mistrust me, I'll be gone, my lord.

Edw. No, no ; for, if thou mean'st to murder me,
Thou wilt return again ; and therefore stay.   [*Sleeps.*

Light. He sleeps.   [*a while !*

Edw. [*waking*] O, let me not die yet ! O, stay

Light. How now, my lord !

Edw. Something still buzzeth in mine ears,
And tells me, if I sleep, I never wake : '
This fear is that which makes me tremble thus;
And therefore tell me, wherefore art thou come ?

Light. To rid thee of thy life.—Matrevis, come !

Enter MATREVIS *and* GURNEY.

Edw. I am too weak and feeble to resist.—
Assist me, sweet God, and receive my soul !

Light. Run for the table.

Edw. O, spare me, or despatch me in a trice !
        [MATREVIS *brings in a table.*   KING EDWARD
            *is murdered by holding him down on the
            bed with the table, and stamping on it.*

Light. So, lay the table down, and stamp on it,
But not too hard, lest that thou bruise his body.

Mat. I fear me that this cry will raise the town,
And therefore let us take horse and away.

Light. Tell me, sirs, was it not bravely done ?

Gur. Excellent well : take this for thy reward.
                    [*Stabs* LIGHTBORN, *who dies.*

Come, let us cast the body in the moat,
And bear the king's to Mortimer our lord :
Away !   [*Exeunt with the bodies.*

SCENE VI.

Enter MORTIMER *and* MATREVIS.

Y. Mor. Is't done, Matrevis, and the murderer dead?
Mat. Aye, my good lord ; I would it were undone.
Y. Mor. Matrevis, if thou now growest penitent
I'll be thy ghostly father ; therefore chuse,
Whether thou wilt be secret in this,
Or else die by the hand of Mortimer.
Mat. Gurney, my lord, is fled, and will, I fear,
Betray us both, therefore let me fly.
Y. Mor. Fly to the savages.
Mat. I humbly thank your honour.
Y. Mor. As for myself, I stand as Jove's huge tree ;
And others are but shrubs compared to me.
All tremble at my name, and I fear none ;
Let's see who dare impeach me for his death.

Enter the QUEEN.

Queen. Ah, Mortimer, the king my son hath news
His father's dead, and we have murdered him.
Y. Mor. What if he have ? the king is yet a child.
Queen. Aye, but he tears his hair, and wrings his
    hands,
And vows to be revenged upon us both.
Into the council-chamber he is gone,
To crave the aid and succour of his peers.
Ah me ! see where he comes, and they with him ;
Now, Mortimer, begins our tragedy.

Enter the KING, *with the* LORDS.

First Lord. Fear not, my lord, know that you are a
 king.
King. Villain !
Y. Mor. How now, my lord ?
King. Think not that I am frighted with thy
 words !
My father's murdered through thy treachery ;
And thou shalt die, and on his mournful hearse
Thy hateful and accursed head shall lie,
To witness to the world, that by thy means
His kingly body was too soon interred.
 Queen. Weep not, sweet son !
King. Forbid me not to weep, he was my father ;
And, had you loved him half so well as I,
You could not bear his death thus patiently.
But you, I fear, conspired with Mortimer.
 Lords. Why speak you not unto my lord the king ?
Y. Mor. Because I think scorn to be accused.
Who is the man dare say I murdered him ?
 King. Traitor ! in me my loving father speaks,
And plainly saith, 'twas thou that murder'dst him.
 Y. Mor. But hath your grace no other proof than
 this ?
King. Yes, if this be the hand of Mortimer.
Y. Mor. False Gurney hath betrayed me and him-
 self.   [*Aside.*
Queen. I feared as much ; murder cannot be hid.
                                     [*Aside.*
Y. Mor. 'Tis my hand ; what gather you by this ?
King. That thither thou didst send a murderer.
Y. Mor. What murderer ? Bring forth the man I
 sent.

King. Aye, Mortimer, thou know'st that he is
   slain ;
And so shalt thou be too. Why stays he here ?
Bring him unto a hurdle, drag him forth,
Hang him, I say, and set his quarters up.
But bring his head back presently to me.
   Queen. For my sake, sweet son, pity Mortimer.
   Y. Mor. Madam, entreat not, I will rather die,
Than sue for life unto a paltry boy.
   King. Hence with the traitor ! with the murderer !
   Y. Mor. Base Fortune, now I see, that in thy wheel
There is a point, to which when men aspire,
They tumble headlong down : that point I touched,
And, seeing there was no place to mount up higher,
Why should I grieve at my declining fall ?
Farewell, fair queen ; weep not for Mortimer,
That scorns the world, and, as a traveller,
Goes to discover countries yet unknown.
   King. What ! suffer you the traitor to delay ?
                              [Mortimer *is taken away.*
   Queen. As thou receivedest thy life from me,
Spill not the blood of gentle Mortimer.
   King. This argues that you spilt my father's blood,
Else would you not entreat for Mortimer.
   Queen. I spill his blood ? no.
   King. Aye, madam, you ; for so the rumour runs.
   Queen. That rumour is untrue ; for loving thee,
Is this report raised on poor Isabel ?
   King. I do not think her so unnatural.
   Second Lord. My lord, I fear me it will prove too
   true.
   King. Mother, you are suspected for his death,
And therefore we commit you to the Tower,
Till farther trial may be made thereof ;

If you be guilty, though I be your son,
Think not to find me slack or pitiful.

Queen. Nay, to my death, for too long have I lived,
Whenas my son thinks to abridge my days.

King. Away with her, her words enforce these tears,
And I shall pity her if she speak again.

Queen. Shall I not mourn for my beloved lord,
And with the rest accompany him to his grave?

Lord. Thus, madam, 'tis the king's will you shall
    hence.

Queen. He hath forgotten me; stay, I am his
    mother.

Lord. That boots not; therefore, gentle madam, go.

Queen. Then come, sweet death, and rid me of this
    grief.   [*Exit.*

Re-enter a Lord, *with the head of* MORTIMER.

Lord. My lord, here is the head of Mortimer.

King. Go fetch my father's hearse, where it shall lie;
And bring my funeral robes. Accursed head,
Could I have ruled thee then, as I do now,
Thou had'st not hatched this monstrous treachery.
Here comes the hearse; help me to mourn, my lords.
Sweet father, here unto thy murdered ghost
I offer up this wicked traitor's head;
And let these tears, distilling from mine eyes,
Be witness of my grief and innocency.   [*Exeunt.*

THE MASSACRE OF PARIS.

GUISE DECLARES HIS POLICY.

ACT I., SCENE 2.

Guise. Now, Guise, begin those deep-engender'd
    thoughts
To burst abroad those never-dying flames
Which cannot be extinguish'd but by blood:
Oft have I levell'd, and at last have learn'd
That peril is the chiefest way to happiness,
And resolution honour's fairest aim.
What glory is there in a common good,
That hangs for every peasant to achieve !
That like I best, that flies beyond my reach.
Set me to scale the high Pyramides,
And thereon set the diadem of France ;
I'll either rend it with my nails to naught,
Or mount the top with my aspiring wings,

Although my downfall be the deepest hell.
For this I wake, when others think I sleep ;
For this I wait, that scorn attendance else ;
For this my quenchless thirst, whereon I build,
Hath often pleaded kindred to the king ;
For this, this head, this heart, this hand, and sword,
Contrives, imagines, and fully executes,
Matters of import aimèd at by many,
Yet understood by none ;
For this, hath heaven engender'd me of earth ;
For this, this earth sustains my body's weight,
And with this weight I'll counterpoise a crown,
Or with seditions weary all the world ;
For this, from Spain the stately Catholics
Send Indian gold to coin me French ecues ;
For this, have I a largess from the Pope,
A pension, and a dispensation too ;
And by that privilege to work upon,
My policy hath fram'd religion.
Religion ! *O Diabole !*
Fie, I am asham'd, however that I seem,
To think a word of such a simple sound,
Of so great matter should be made the ground.
The gentle king, whose pleasure uncontroll'd
Weakeneth his body, and will waste his realm,
If I repair not what he ruinates—
Him, as a child, I daily win with words,
So that for proof he barely bears the name ;
I execute, and he sustains the blame.

The Mother-Queen works wonders for my sake,
And in my love entombs the hope of France,
Rifling the bowels of her treasury,
To supply my wants and necessity.
Paris hath full five hundred colleges,
As monasteries, priories, abbeys, and halls,
Wherein are thirty thousand able men,
Besides a thousand sturdy student Catholics ;
And more—of my knowledge, in one cloister keep
Five hundred fat Franciscan friars and priests :
All this, and more, if more may be compris'd,
To bring the will of our desires to end.
Then, Guise,
Since thou hast all the cards within thy hands,
To shuffle or cut, take this as surest thing,
That, right or wrong, thou deal thyself a king —
Ay, but, Navarre—'tis but a nook of France,
Sufficient yet for such a petty king,
That, with a rabblement of his heretics,
Blinds Europe's eyes, and troubleth our estate.
Him will we—[*Pointing to his sword.*] but first let's
    follow those in France
That hinder our possession to the crown.
As Cæsar to his soldiers, so say I—
Those that hate me will I learn to loathe.
Give me a look, that, when I bend the brows,
Pale death may walk in furrows of my face ;
A hand, that with a grasp may gripe the world ;
An ear to hear what my detractors say ;

A royal seat, a sceptre, and a crown ;
That those which do behold them may become
As men that stand and gaze against the sun.
The plot is laid, and things shall come to pass
Where resolution strives for victory.

THE DEATH OF GUISE.

Act III., Scene 2.

Guise. Now sues the king for favour to the Guise,
And all his minions stoop when I command :
Why, this 'tis to have an army in the field.
Now, by the holy sacrament, I swear,
As ancient Romans o'er their captive lords,
So will I triumph o'er this wanton king ;
And he shall follow my proud chariot's wheels.
Now do I but begin to look about,
And all my former time was spent in vain.
Hold, sword,
For in thee is the Duke of Guise's hope.

Re-enter Third Murderer.

Villain, why dost thou look so ghastly ? speak.
    Third Murd. O, pardon me, my Lord of Guise !
    Guise. Pardon thee ! why, what hast thou done ?
    Third Murd. O my lord, I am one of them that is
set to murder you !
    Guise. To murder me, villain !
    Third Murd. Ay, my lord : the rest have ta'en their

standings in the next room ; therefore, good my lord,
go not forth.

Guise. Yet Cæsar shall go forth.
Let mean conceits and baser men fear death :
Tut, they are peasants ; I am Duke of Guise ;
And princes with their looks engender fear.

First Murd. [*within.*] Stand close ; he is coming ;
I know him by his voice.

Guise. As pale as ashes ! nay, then, it is time
To look about.

Enter First *and* Second Murderers.

First and Sec. Murderers. Down with him, down
with him !   [*They stab* GUISE.

Guise. O, I have my death's wound ! give me leave
to speak.

Sec. Murd. Then pray to God, and ask forgiveness
of the king.

Guise. Trouble me not ; I ne'er offended him,
Nor will I ask forgiveness of the king.
O, that I have not power to stay my life,
Nor immortality to be reveng'd !
To die by peasants, what a grief is this !
Ah, Sixtus, be reveng'd upon the king !
Philip and Parma, I am slain for you !
Pope, excommunicate, Philip, depose
The wicked branch of curs'd Valois his line !
Vive la messe! perish Huguenots !
Thus Cæsar did go forth, and thus he died.   [*Dies.*
(K)

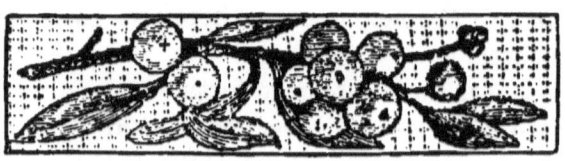

DIDO, QUEEN OF CARTHAGE.

A VISION OF OLYMPUS.

ACT I., SCENE 1.

Here the curtains draw: there is discovered JUPITER *dandling* GANYMEDE *on his knee, and* HERMES *lying asleep.*

Jup. Come, gentle Ganymede, and play with me ;
I love thee well, say Juno what she will.

Gan. I am much better for your worthless love,
That will not shield me from her shrewish blows !
To-day, whenas I fill'd into your cups,
And held the cloth of pleasance whiles you drank,
She reach'd me such a rap for that I spill'd,
As made the blood run down mine ears.

Jup. What, dares she strike the darling of my
thoughts ?
By Saturn's soul, and this earth-threatening hair,

That, shaken thrice, makes nature's buildings quake,
I vow, if she but once frown on thee more,
To hang her, meteor-like, 'twixt heaven and earth,
And bind her, hand and foot, with golden cords,
As once I did for harming Hercules!
Gan. Might I but see that pretty sport a-foot,
O, how would I with Helen's brother laugh,
And bring the Gods to wonder at the game!
Sweet Jupiter, if e'er I pleas'd thine eye,
Or seemèd fair, wall'd in with eagle's wings,
Grace my immortal beauty with this boon,
And I will spend my time in thy bright arms.
Jup. What is't, sweet wag, I should deny thy youth?
Whose face reflects such pleasure to mine eyes,
As I, exhal'd with thy fire-darting beams,
Have oft driven back the horses of the Night,
Whenas they would have hal'd thee from my sight.
Sit on my knee, and call for thy content,
Control proud Fate, and cut the thread of Time :
Why, are not all the gods at thy command,
And heaven and earth the bounds of thy delight?
Vulcan shall dance to make thee laughing-sport,
And my nine daughters sing when thou art sad;
From Juno's bird I'll pluck her spotted pride,
To make thee fans wherewith to cool thy face ;
And Venus' swans shall shed their silver down,
To sweeten out the slumbers of thy bed ;
Hermes no more shall show the world his wings,
If that thy fancy in his feathers dwell,

But, as this one, I'll tear them all from him,

[*Plucks a feather from* HERMES' *wings.*

Do thou but say, " their colour pleaseth me."

Hold here, my little love ; these linkèd gems,

[*Gives jewels.*

My Juno ware upon her marriage-day,

Put thou about thy neck, my own sweet heart,

And trick thy arms and shoulders with my theft.

Gan. I would have a jewel for mine ear,

And a fine brooch to put in my hat,

And then I'll hug with you an hundred times.

Jup. And shalt have, Ganymede, if thou wilt be my
love.

Enter VENUS.

Ven. Ay, this is it : you can sit toying there,

And playing with that female wanton boy,

Whiles my Æneas wanders on the seas,

And rests a prey to every billow's pride.

Juno, false Juno, in her chariot's pomp,

Drawn through the heavens by steeds of Boreas' brood,

Made Hebe to direct her airy wheels

Into the windy country of the clouds ;

Where, finding Æolus entrench'd with storms,

And guarded with a thousand grisly ghosts,

She humbly did beseech him for our bane,

And charg'd him drown my son with all his train.

Then gan the winds break ope their brazen doors,

And all Æolia to be up in arms :

Poor Troy must now be sack'd upon the sea,
And Neptune's waves be envious men of war ;
Epeus' horse, to Ætna's hill transform'd,
Preparèd stands to wreck their wooden walls ;
And Æolus, like Agamemnon, sounds
The surges, his fierce soldiers, to the spoil ;
See how the night, Ulysses-like, comes forth,
And intercepts the day, as Dolon erst !
Ay, me ! the stars suppris'd, like Rhesus' steeds,
Are drawn by darkness forth Astræus' tents.
What shall I do to save thee, my sweet boy ?
Whenas the waves do threat our crystal world,
And Proteus, raising hills of flood on high,
Intends, ere long, to sport him in the sky.
False Jupiter, reward'st thou virtue so ?
What, is not piety exempt from woe ?
Then die, Æneas, in thine innocence,
Since that religion hath no recompense.

Jup. Content thee, Cytherea, in thy care,
Since thy Æneas' wandering fate is firm,
Whose weary limbs shall shortly make repose
In those fair walls I promis'd him of yore.
But, first in blood must his good fortune bud,
Before he be the lord of Turnus' town,
Or force her smile that hitherto hath frown'd :
Three winters shall he with the Rutiles war,
And, in the end, subdue them with his sword ;
And full three summers likewise shall he waste
In managing those fierce barbarian minds ;

Which once perform'd, poor Troy, so long sup-
   press'd,
From forth her ashes shall advance her head,
And flourish once again, that erst was dead.
But bright Ascanius, beauty's better work,
Who with the sun divides one radiant shape,
Shall build his throne amidst those starry towers
That earth-born Atlas, groaning, underprops :
No bounds, but heaven, shall bound his empery,
Whose azur'd gates, enchasèd with his name,
Shall make the Morning haste her grey uprise,
To feed her eyes with his engraven fame.
Thus, in stout Hector's race, three hundred years
The Roman sceptre royal shall remain,
Till that a princess-priest, conceiv'd by Mars,
Shall yield to dignity a double birth,
Who will eternish Troy in their attempts.

   Ven. How may I credit these thy flattering terms,
When yet both sea and sands beset their ships,
And Phœbus, as in Stygian pools, refrains
To taint his tresses in the Tyrrhene main ?

   Jup. I will take order for that presently.—
Hermes, awake ! and haste to Neptune's realm,
Whereas the wind-god, warring now with fate,
Besiege[s] th' offspring of our kingly loins :
Charge him from me to turn his stormy powers,
And fetter them in Vulcan's sturdy brass,
That durst thus proudly wrong our kinsman's peace.
                    [*Exit* HERMES.

Venus, farewell : thy son shall be our care.—
Come, Ganymede, we must about this gear.

[Exeunt JUPITER *and* GANYMEDE.

THE FALL OF TROY.

ACT II., SCENE 1.

Dido. Nay, leave not here ; resolve me of the rest.

Æn. O, the enchanting words of that base slave
Made him to think Epeus' pine-tree horse
A sacrifice to appease Minerva's wrath !
The rather, that for one Laocoon,
Breaking a spear upon his hollow breast,
Was with two-wingèd serpents stung to death.
Whereat aghast, we were commanded straight
With reverence to draw it into Troy :
In which unhappy work was I employ'd ;
These hands did help to hale it to the gates,
Through which it could not enter, 'twas so huge—
O, had it never enter'd, Troy had stood !
But Priamus, impatient of delay,
Enforc'd a wide breach in that rampir'd wall
Which thousand battering rams could never pierce,
And so came in this fatal instrument ·
At whose accursed feet, as overjoy'd,
We banqueted, till, overcome with wine,
Some surfeited, and others soundly slept.
Which Sinon viewing, caused the Greekish spies

To haste to Tenedos, and tell the camp :
Then he unlocked the horse ; and suddenly,
From out his entrails, Neoptolemus,
Setting his spear upon the ground, leapt forth,
And, after him, a thousand Grecians more,
In whose stern faces shin'd the quenchless fire
That after burnt the pride of Asia.
By this, the camp was come unto the walls,
And through the breach did march into the streets,
Where, meeting with the rest, "Kill, kill !" they
    cried.
Frighted with this confusèd noise, I rose,
And, looking from a turret, might behold
Young infants swimming in their parents' blood,
Headless carcasses piled up in heaps,
Virgins half-dead, dragg'd by their golden hair,
And with main force flung on a ring of pikes,
Old men with swords thrust through their aged sides,
Kneeling for mercy to a Greekish lad,
Who with steel pole-axes dash'd out their brains.
Then buckled I mine armour, drew my sword,
And thinking to go down, came Hector's ghost,
With ashy visage, blueish sulphur eyes,
His arms torn from his shoulders, and his breast
Furrow'd with wounds, and, that which made me weep,
Thongs at his heels, by which Achilles' horse
Drew him in triumph through the Greekish camp,
Burst from the earth, crying, "Æneas, fly !
Troy is a-fire, the Grecians have the town !"

Dido. O Hector, who weeps not to hear thy name ?
Æn. Yet flung I forth, and desperate of my life,
Ran in the thickest throngs, and with this sword
Sent many of their savage ghosts to hell.
At last came Pyrrhus, fell and full of ire,
His harness dropping blood, and on his spear
The mangled head of Priam's youngest son ;
And, after him, his band of Myrmidons,
With balls of wild-fire in their murdering paws,
Which made the funeral flame that burnt fair Troy ;
All which hemm'd me about, crying, " This is he ! "
   Dido. Ah, how could poor Æneas scape their hands ?
   Æn. My mother Venus, jealous of my health,
Convey'd me from their crookèd nets and bands ;
So I escap'd the furious Pyrrhus' wrath :
Who then ran to the palace of the king,
And at Jove's altar finding Priamus,
About whose withered neck hung Hecuba,
Folding his hand in hers, and jointly both
Beating their breasts, and falling on the ground,
He, with his falchion's point raised up at once,
And with Megæra's eyes, star'd in their face,
Threatening a thousand deaths at every glance :
To whom the agèd king thus, trembling, spoke ;
" Achilles' son, remember what I was,
Father of fifty sons, but they are slain ;
Lord of my fortune, but my fortune's turn'd ;
King of this city, but my Troy is fir'd ;
And now am neither father, lord, nor king :

Yet who so wretched but desires to live ?
O, let me live, great Neoptolemus !"
Not mov'd at all, but smiling at his tears,
This butcher, whilst his hands were yet held up,
Treading upon his breast, struck off his hands.
    Dido. O, end Æneas ! I can hear no more.
    Æn. At which the frantic queen leap'd on his face,
And in his eyelids hanging by the nails,
A little while prolong'd her husband's life.
At last, the soldiers pulled her by the heels,
And swung her howling in the empty air,
Which sent an echo to the wounded king :
Whereat he lifted up his bed-rid limbs,
And would have grappled with Achilles' son,
Forgetting both his want of strength and hands ;
Which he disdaining, whisk'd his sword about,
And with the wind thereof the king fell down ;
Then from the navel to the throat at once
He ripp'd old Priam ; at whose latter gasp
Jove's marble statue gan to bend the brow,
As loathing Pyrrhus for this wicked act.
Yet he, undaunted, took his father's flag,
And dipp'd it in the old king's chill-cold blood,
And then in triumph ran into the streets,
Through which he could not pass for slaughtered men ;
So, leaning on his sword, he stood stone-still,
Viewing the fire wherewith rich Ilion burnt.
By this, I got my father on my back,
This young boy in mine arms, and by the hand

Led fair Creusa, my belovèd wife ;
When thou, Achates, with thy sword mad'st way,
And we were round environ'd with the Greeks :
O, there I lost my wife ! and, had not we
Fought manfully, I had not told this tale.
Yet manhood would not serve ; of force we fled ;
And, as we went unto our ships, thou know'st
We saw Cassandra sprawling in the streets,
Whom Ajax ravish'd in Diana's fane,
Her cheeks swollen with sighs, her hair all rent ;
Whom I took up to bear unto our ships ;
But suddenly the Grecians follow'd us,
And I, alas, was forc'd to let her lie !
Than got we to our ships, and, being aboard,
Polyxena cried out, " Æneas, stay !
The Greeks pursue me ; stay, and take me in !"
Mov'd with her voice, I leap'd into the sea,
Thinking to bear her on my back aboard,
For all our ships were launched into the deep,
And, as I swom, she, standing on the shore,
Was by the cruel Myrmidons surpris'd,
And, after that, by Pyrrhus sacrific'd.

DIDO REVEALS HER LOVE.

ACT III., SCENE 2.

Dido. O dull, conceited Dido, that till now
Didst never think Æneas beautiful !
But now, for quittance of this oversight,

I'll make me bracelets of his golden hair ;
His glistering eyes shall be my looking-glass ;
His lips an altar, where I'll offer up
As many kisses as the sea hath sands ;
Instead of music I will hear him speak ;
His looks shall be my only library ;
And thou, Æneas, Dido's treasury,
In whose fair bosom I will lock more wealth
Than twenty thousand Indias can afford.
O, here he comes ! Love, love, give Dido leave
To be more modest than her thoughts admit,
Lest I be made a wonder to the world.

Enter Æneas, Achates, Sergestus, Ilioneus, *and*
Cloanthus.

Achates, how doth Carthage please your lord ?
    Ach. That will Æneas shew your majesty.
    Dido. Æneas, art thou there ?
    Æn. I understand, your highness sent for me.
    Dido. No ; but, now thou art here, tell me, in
        sooth,
In what might Dido highly pleasure thee.
    Æn. So much have I receiv'd at Dido's hands,
As, without blushing, I can ask no more :
Yet, queen of Afric, are my ships unrigg'd,
My sails all rent in sunder with the wind,
My oars broken, and my tackling lost,
Yea, all my navy split with rocks and shelves ;

Nor stern nor anchor have our maimèd fleet ;
Our masts the furious winds struck overboard :
Which piteous wants if Dido will supply,
We will account her author of our lives.
  Dido. Æneas, I'll repair thy Trojan ships,
Conditionally that thou wilt stay with me,
And let Achates sail to Italy :
I'll give thee tackling made of rivell'd gold,
Wound on the barks of odoriferous trees ;
Oars of massy ivory, full of holes,
Through which the water shall delight to play ;
Thy anchors shall be hew'd from crystal rocks,
Which, if thou lose, shall shine above the waves ;
The masts, whereon thy swelling sails shall hang,
Hollow pyramides of silver plate ;
The sails of folded lawn, where shall be wrought
The wars of Troy—but not Troy's overthrow ;
For ballass, empty Dido's treasury :
Take what ye will, but leave Æneas here.
Achates, thou shalt be so seemly clad,
As sea-born nymphs shall swarm about thy ships,
And wanton mermaids court thee with sweet songs,
Flinging in favours of more sovereign worth
Than Thetis hangs about Apollo's neck,
So that Æneas may but stay with me.

DIDO DREADS HER LOVER'S DEPARTURE.

Act IV., Scene 4.

Dido. Speaks not Æneas like a conqueror ?
O blessèd tempests that did drive him in !
O happy sand that made him run aground !
Henceforth you shall be our Carthage gods.
Ay, but it may be, he will leave my love,
And seek a foreign land call'd Italy :
O, that I had a charm to keep the winds
Within the closure of a golden ball ;
Or that the Tyrrhene sea were in mine arms,
That he might suffer shipwreck on my breast,
As oft as he attempts to hoist up sail !
I must prevent him ; wishing will not serve.—
Go bid my nurse take young Ascanius,
And bear him in the country to her house ;
Æneas will not go without his son;
Yet, lest he should, for I am full of fear,
Bring me his oars, his tackling, and his sails.
                            [*Exit* First Lord.
What if I sink his ships ? O, he will frown !
Better he frown than I should die for grief.
I cannot see him frown ; it may not be :
Armies of foes resolv'd to win this town,
Or impious traitors vow'd to have my life,
Affright me not ; only Æneas' frown
Is that which terrifies poor Dido's heart :

Not bloody spears, appearing in the air,
Presage the downfall of my empery,
Nor blazing comets threatened Dido's death ;
It is Æneas' frown that ends my days.
If he forsake me not, I never die ;
For in his looks I see eternity,
And he'll make me immortal with a kiss.

THE NURSE AS TEMPTRESS.
ACT IV., SCENE 5.

Enter Nurse, *with* CUPID *as* ASCANIUS.

Nurse. My Lord Ascanius, you must go with me.
Cup. Whither must I go ? I'll stay with my mother.
Nurse. No, thou shalt go with me unto my house.
I have an orchard that hath store of plums,
Brown almonds, services, ripe figs, and dates,
Dewberries, apples, yellow oranges ;
A garden where are bee-hives full of honey,
Musk-roses, and a thousand sort of flowers ;
And in the midst doth run a silver stream,
Where thou shalt see the red-gill'd fishes leap,
White swans, and many lovely water-fowls.
Now speak, Ascanius, will you go or no ?
   Cup. Come, come, I'll go. How far hence is your
     house ?
   Nurse. But hereby, child ; we shall get thither
     straight.

Cup. Nurse, I am weary ; will you carry me ?
Nurse. Ay, so you'll dwell with me, and call me
    mother.
Cup. So you'll love me, I care not if I do.
Nurse. That I might live to see this boy a man !
How prettily he laughs ! Go, you wag !
You'll be a twigger when you come to age.—
Say Dido what she will, I am not old ;
I'll be no more a widow ; I am young ;
I'll have a husband, or else a lover.
    Cup. A husband, and no teeth !

DIDO'S DESPAIR.

Act V., Scene 2.

    Dido. Hast thou forgot how many neighbour kings
Were up in arms, for making thee my love ?
How Carthage did rebel, Iarbas storm,
And all the world call'd me a second Helen,
For being entangled by a stranger's looks ?
So thou wouldst prove as true as Paris did,
Would, as fair Troy was, Carthage might be sack'd,
And I be call'd a second Helena !
Had I a son by thee, the grief were less,
That I might see Æneas in his face :
Now if thou go'st, what canst thou leave behind,
But rather will augment than ease my woe ?

Æn. In vain, my love, thou spend'st thy fainting
    breath :
If words might move me, I were overcome.
  Dido. And wilt thou not be mov'd with Dido's
    words ?
Thy mother was no goddess, perjur'd man,
Nor Dardanus the author of thy stock ;
But thou art sprung from Scythian Caucasus,
And tigers of Hyrcania gave thee suck.—
Ah, foolish Dido, to forbear this long !—
Wast thou not wreck'd upon this Libyan shore,
And cam'st to Dido like a fisher swain ?
Repair'd not I thy ships, made thee a king,
And all thy needy followers noblemen ?
O serpent, that came creeping from the shore,
And I for pity harbour'd in my bosom,
Wilt thou now slay me with thy venom'd sting,
And hiss at Dido for preserving thee ?
Go, go, and spare not ; seek out Italy :
I hope that that which love forbids me do,
The rocks and sea-gulfs will perform at large,
And thou shalt perish in the billows' ways,
To whom poor Dido doth bequeath revenge :
Ay, traitor ! and the waves shall cast thee up,
Where thou and false Achates first set foot ;
Which if it chance, I'll give ye burial,
And weep upon your lifeless carcasses,
Though thou nor he will pity me a whit.
Why star'st thou in my face ? If thou wilt stay,
           (L)

Leap in mine arms ; mine arms are open wide ;
If not, turn from me, and I'll turn from thee ;
For though thou hast the heart to say farewell,
I have not power to stay thee.   [*Exit* ÆNEAS.
                       Is he gone ?
Ay, but he'll come again ; he cannot go ;
He loves me too-too well to serve me so :
Yet he that in my sight would not relent,
Will, being absent, be obdurate still.
By this, he has got to the water-side ;
And, see, the sailors take him by the hand ;
But he shrinks back ; and now, remembering me,
Returns amain : welcome, welcome, my love !
But where's Æneas ? ah, he's gone, he's gone !

   .   .   .   .   .

   Dido. O Anna, Anna, I will follow him !
   Anna. How can you go, when he hath all your fleet ?
   Dido. I'll frame me wings of wax, like Icarus,
And, o'er his ships, will soar unto the sun,
That they may melt, and I fall in his arms ;
Or else I'll make a prayer unto the waves,
That I may swim to him, like Triton's niece.
O Anna, fetch Arion's harp,
That I may tice a dolphin to the shore,
And ride upon his back unto my love !
Look, sister, look! lovely Æneas' ships !
See, see, the billows heave 'em up to heaven,
And now down fall the keels into the deep !
O sister, sister, take away the rocks !

They'll break his ships.   O Proteus, Neptune, Jove,
Save, save Æneas, Dido's liefest love !
Now is he come on shore, safe without hurt :
But, see, Achates wills him put to sea,
And all the sailors merry-make for joy ;
But he, remembering me, shrinks back again :
See, where he comes ! welcome, welcome, my love
     Anna. Ah, sister, leave these idle fantasies !
Sweet sister, cease ; remember who you are.
     Dido. Dido I am, unless I be deceiv'd :
And must I rave thus for a runagate ?
Must I make ships for him to sail away ?
Nothing can bear me to him but a ship,
And he hath all my fleet.   What shall I do,
But die in fury of this oversight ?
Ay, I must be the murderer of myself ;
No, but I am not ; yet I will be straight.

HERO AND LEANDER.

THE FIRST SESTIAD.

The Argument of the First Sestiad.

Hero's description and her love's:
The fane of Venus, where he moves
His worthy love-suit, and attains;
Whose bliss the wrath of Fates restrains
For Cupid's grace to Mercury:
Which tale the author doth imply.

ON Hellespont, guilty of true love's blood,
 In view and opposite two cities stood,
Sea-borderers, disjoin'd by Neptune's might;
The one Abydos, the other Sestos hight.
At Sestos Hero dwelt; Hero the fair,
Whom young Apollo courted for her hair,
And offer'd as a dower his burning throne,
Where she should sit, for men to gaze upon.

The outside of her garments were of lawn,
The lining purple silk, with gilt stars drawn ;
Her wide sleeves green, and border'd with a grove,
Where Venus in her naked glory strove
To please the careless and disdainful eyes
Of proud Adonis, that before her lies ;
Her kirtle blue, whereon was many a stain,
Made with the blood of wretched lovers slain.
Upon her head she ware a myrtle wreath,
From whence her veil reach'd to the ground beneath :
Her veil was artificial flowers and leaves,
Whose workmanship both man and beast deceives :
Many would praise the sweet smell as she past,
When 'twas the odour which her breath forth cast ;
And there for honey bees have sought in vain,
And, beat from thence, have lighted there again.
About her neck hung chains of pebble-stone,
Which, lighten'd by her neck, like diamonds shone.
She ware no gloves ; for neither sun nor wind
Would burn or parch her hands, but, to her mind,
Or warm or cool them, for they took delight
To play upon those hands, they were so white.
Buskins of shells, all silver'd, usèd she,
And branch'd with blushing coral to the knee ;
Where sparrows perch'd, of hollow pearl and gold,
Such as the world would wonder to behold :
Those with sweet water oft her handmaid fills,
Which, as she went, would cherup through the bills.
Some say, for her the fairest Cupid pin'd,

And, looking in her face, was strooken blind.
But this is true ; so like was one the other,
As he imagin'd Hero was his mother ;
And oftentimes into her bosom flew,
About her naked neck his bare arms threw,
And laid his childish head upon her breast,
And, with still panting rock, there took his rest.
So lovely-fair was Hero, Venus' nun,
As Nature wept, thinking she was undone,
Because she took more from her than she left,
And of such wondrous beauty her bereft :
Therefore, in sign her treasure suffer'd wrack,
Since Hero's time hath half the world been black.
  Amorous Leander, beautiful and young
(Whose tragedy divine Musæus sung),
Dwelt at Abydos ; since him dwelt there none
For whom succeeding times make greater moan.
His dangling tresses, that were never shorn,
Had they been cut, and unto Colchos borne,
Would have allured the venturous youth of Greece
To hazard more than for the golden fleece.
Fair Cynthia wish'd his arms might be her sphere ;
Grief makes her pale, because she moves not there.
His body was as straight as Circe's wand ;
Jove might have sipt out nectar from his hand.
Even as delicious meat is to the tast,
So was his neck in touching, and surpast
The white of Pelop's shoulder : I could tell ye,
How smooth his breast was, and how white his belly ;

And whose immortal fingers did imprint
That heavenly path with many a curious dint
That runs along his back ; but my rude pen
Can hardly blazon forth the loves of men,
Much less of powerful gods : let it suffice
That my slack Muse sings of Leander's eyes ;
Those orient cheeks and lips, exceeding his
That leapt into the water for a kiss
Of his own shadow, and, despising many,
Died ere he could enjoy the love of any.
Had wild Hippolytus Leander seen,
Enamour'd of his beauty had he been :
His presence made the rudest peasant melt,
That in the vast uplandish country dwelt :
The barbarous Thracian soldier, mov'd with nought,
Was mov'd with him, and for his favour sought.
Some swore he was a maid in man's attire,
For in his looks were all that men desire—
A pleasant-smiling cheek, a speaking eye,
A brow for love to banquet royally ;
And such as knew he was a man, would say,
" Leander, thou art made for amorous play :
Why art thou not in love, and lov'd of all ?
Though thou be fair, yet be not thine own thrall."
    The men of wealthy Sestos every year,
For his sake whom their goddess held so dear,
Rose-cheek'd Adonis, kept a solemn feast :
Thither resorted many a wandering guest
To meet their loves : such as had none at all,

Came lovers home from this great festival ;
For every street, like to a firmament,
Glister'd with breathing stars, who, where they went,
Frighted the melancholy earth, which deem'd
Eternal heaven to burn, for so it seem'd,
As if another Phaëton had got
The guidance of the sun's rich chariot.
But, far above the loveliest, Hero shin'd,
And stole away th' enchanted gazer's mind ;
For like sea-nymphs' inveigling harmony,
So was her beauty to the standers by ;
Nor that night-wandering, pale, and watery star
(When yawning dragons draw her thirling car
From Latmus' mount up to the gloomy sky,
Where, crown'd with blazing light and majesty
She proudly sits) more overrules the flood
Than she the hearts of those that near her stood.
Even as when gaudy nymphs pursue the chase,
Wretched Ixion's shaggy-footed race,
Incens'd with savage heat, gallop amain
From steep pine-bearing mountains to the plain,
So ran the people forth to gaze upon her,
And all that view'd her were enamour'd on her :
And as in fury of a dreadful fight,
Their fellows being slain or put to flight,
Poor soldiers stand with fear of death dead-strooken,
So at her presence all surpris'd and tooken,
Await the sentence of her scornful eyes ;
He whom she favours lives ; the other dies :

There might you see one sigh ; another rage ;
And some, their violent passions to assuage,
Compile sharp satires ; but, alas, too late !
For faithful love will never turn to hate ;
And many, seeing great princes were denied,
Pin'd as they went, and thinking on her died.
On this feast-day—Oh, cursèd day and hour !
Went Hero thorough Sestos, from her tower
To Venus' temple, where unhappily,
As after chanc'd, they did each other spy.
So fair a church as this had Venus none :
The walls were of discolour'd jasper-stone,
Wherein was Proteus carv'd ; and overhead
A lively vine of green sea-agate spread,
Where by one hand light-headed Bacchus hung,
And with the other wine from grapes outwrung.
Of crystal shining fair the pavement was ;
The town of Sestos call'd it Venus' glass :
There might you see the gods, in sundry shapes,
Committing heady riots, incest, rapes ;
For know, that underneath this radiant flour
Was Danäe's statue in a brazen tower ;
Jove slily stealing from his sister's bed,
To dally with Idalian Ganymed,
And for his love Europa bellowing loud,
And tumbling with the Rainbow in a cloud ;
Blood-quaffing Mars heaving the iron net
Which limping Vulcan and his Cyclops set ;
Love kindling fire, to burn such towns as Troy ;

Silvanus weeping for the lovely boy
That now is turn'd into a cypress-tree,
Under whose shade the wood-gods love to be.
And in the midst a silver altar stood :
There Hero, sacrificing turtles' blood,
Vail'd to the ground, veiling her eyelids close ;
And modestly they open'd as she rose :
Thence flew Love's arrow with the golden head ;
And thus Leander was enamourèd.
Stone-still he stood, and evermore he gaz'd,
Till with the fire, that from his countenance blaz'd,
Relenting Hero's gentle heart was strook :
Such force and virtue hath an amorous look.
    It lies not in our power to love or hate,
For will in us is overrul'd by fate.
When two are stript long ere the course begin,
We wish that one should lose, the other win ;
And one especially do we affect
Of two gold ingots, like in each respect :
The reason no man knows ; let it suffice,
What we behold is censur'd by our eyes.
Where both deliberate, the love is slight :
Who ever lov'd, that lov'd not at first sight ?
    He kneel'd ; but unto her devoutly pray'd :
Chaste Hero to herself thus softly said,
" Were I the saint he worships, I would hear him ; "
And, as she spake those words, came somewhat near
        him.
He started up ; she blush'd as one asham'd ;

Wherewith Leander much more was inflam'd.
He touch'd her hand ; in touching it she trembled :
Love deeply grounded, hardly is dissembled,
These lovers parled by the touch of hands :
True love is mute, and oft amazèd stands.
Thus while dumb signs their yielding hearts entangled,
The air with sparks of living fire was spangled :
And Night, deep-drench'd in misty Acheron,
Heav'd up her head, and half the world upon
Breath'd darkness forth (dark night is Cupid's day) :
And now begins Leander to display
Love's holy fire, with words, with sighs, and tears ;
Which, like sweet music, enter'd Hero's ears ;
And yet at every word she turn'd aside,
And always cut him off, as he replied.
At last, like to a bold sharp sophister,
With cheerful hope thus he accosted her :
" Fair creature, let me speak without offence :
I would my rude words had the influence
To lead thy thoughts as thy fair looks do mine !
Then shouldst thou be his prisoner, who is thine.
Be not unkind and fair ; misshapen stuff
Are of behaviour boisterous and rough.
Oh, shun me not, but hear me ere you go !
God knows, I cannot force love as you do :
My words shall be as spotless as my youth,
Full of simplicity and naked truth.
This sacrifice, whose sweet perfume descending
From Venus' altar, to your footsteps bending,

Doth testify that you exceed her far,
To whom you offer, and whose nun you are.
Why should you worship her? her you surpass
As much as sparkling diamonds flaring glass.
A diamond set in lead his worth retains;
A heavenly nymph, belov'd of human swains,
Receives no blemish, but oftimes more grace;
Which makes me hope, although I am but base,
Base in respect of thee divine and pure,
Dutiful service may thy love procure;
And I in duty will excel all other,
As thou in beauty dost exceed Love's mother.
Nor heaven nor thou were made to gaze upon:
As heaven preserves all things, so save thou one.
A stately-builded ship, well rigg'd and tall,
The ocean maketh more majestical:
Why vow'st thou, then, to live in Sestos here,
Who on Love's seas more glorious wouldst appear?
Like untun'd golden strings all women are,
Which long time lie untouch'd, will harshly jar.
Vessels of brass, oft handled, brightly shine:
What difference betwixt the richest mine
And basest mould, but use? for both, not us'd,
Are of like worth. Then treasure is abus'd,
When misers keep it: being put to loan,
In time it will return us two for one.
Rich robes themselves and others do adorn;
Neither themselves nor others, if not worn.
Who builds a palace, and rams up the gate,

Shall see it ruinous and desolate :
Ah, simple Hero, learn thyself to cherish !
Lone women, like to empty houses, perish.
Less sins the poor rich man, that starves himself
In heaping up a mass of drossy pelf,
Than such as you : his golden earth remains,
Which, after his decease, some other gains ;
But this fair gem, sweet in the loss alone,
When you fleet hence, can be bequeath'd to none ;
Or, if it could, down from th' enamell'd sky
All heaven would come to claim this legacy,
And with intestine broils the world destroy,
And quite confound Nature's sweet harmony.
Well therefore by the gods decreed it is,
We human creatures should enjoy that bliss.
One is no number ; maids are nothing, then,
Without the sweet society of men.
Wilt thou live single still ? one shalt thou be,
Though never-singling Hymen couple thee.
Wild savages, that drink of running springs,
Think water far excels all earthly things ;
But they, that daily taste neat wine, despise it :
Virginity, albeit some highly prize it,
Compar'd with marriage, had you tried them both,
Differs as much as wine and water doth.
Base bullion for the stamp's sake we allow :
Even so for men's impression do we you ;
By which alone, our reverend fathers say,
Women receive perfection every way.

This idol, which you term virginity,
Is neither essence subject to the eye,
No, nor to any one exterior sense,
Nor hath it any place of residence,
Nor is't of earth or mould celestial,
Or capable of any form at all.
Of that which hath no being, do not boast :
Things that are not at all, are never lost.
Men foolishly do call it virtuous :
What virtue is it, that is born with us ?
Much less can honour be ascrib'd thereto :
Honour is purchas'd by the deeds we do ;
Believe me, Hero, honour is not won,
Until some honourable deed be done.
Seek you, for chastity, immortal fame,
And know that some have wrong'd Diana's name ?
Whose name is it, if she be false or not,
So she be fair, but some vile tongues will blot ?
But you are fair, ay me ! so wondrous fair,
So young, so gentle, and so debonair,
As Greece will think, if thus you live alone,
Some one or other keeps you as his own.
Then, Hero, hate me not, nor from me fly,
To follow swiftly-blasting infamy.
Perhaps thy secred priesthood makes thee loath :
Tell me to whom mad'st thou that heedless oath ? "
" To Venus," answer'd she ; and, as she spake,
Forth from those two tralucent cisterns brake
A stream of liquid pearl, which down her face

Made milk-white paths, whereon the gods might
  trace
To Jove's high court. He thus replied : "The rites
In which love's beauteous empress most delights,
Are banquets, Doric music, midnight revel,
Plays, masks, and all that stern age counteth evil.
Thee as a holy idiot doth she scorn ;
For thou, in vowing chastity, hast sworn
To rob her name and honour, and thereby
Committ'st a sin far worse than perjury,
Even sacrilege against her deity,
Through regular and formal purity.
To expiate which sin, kiss and shake hands :
Such sacrifice as this Venus demands."
Thereat she smil'd, and did deny him so,
As put thereby, yet might he hope for mo ;
Which makes him quickly reinforce his speech,
And her in humble manner thus beseech :
"Though neither gods nor men may thee deserve,
Yet for her sake, whom you have vow'd to serve,
Abandon fruitless cold virginity,
The gentle queen of love's sole enemy.
Then shall you most resemble Venus' nun,
When Venus' sweet rites are perform'd and done.
Flint-breasted Pallas joys in single life ;
But Pallas and your mistress are at strife.
Love, Hero, then, and be not tyrannous ;
But heal the heart that thou hast wounded thus ;
Nor stain thy youthful years with avarice :

Fair fools delight to be accounted nice.
The richest corn dies, if it be not reapt ;
Beauty alone is lost, too warily kept."
These arguments he us'd, and many more ;
Wherewith she yielded, that was won before.
Hero's looks yielded, but her words made war :
Women are won when they begin to jar.
Thus, having swallow'd Cupid's golden hook,
The more she striv'd, the deeper was she strook :
Yet, evilly feigning anger, strove she still,
And would be thought to grant against her will.
So having paus'd a while, at last she said,
" Who taught thee rhetoric to deceive a maid ?
Ah me ! such words as these should I abhor,
And yet I like them for the orator."
With that, Leander stoop'd to have embrac'd her,
But from his spreading arms away she cast her,
And thus bespake him :   " Gentle youth, forbear
To touch the sacred garments which I wear.
Upon a rock, and underneath a hill,
Far from the town (where all is whist and still,
Save that the sea, playing on yellow sand,
Sends forth a rattling murmur to the land,
Whose sound allures the golden Morpheus
In silence of the night to visit us),
My turret stands ; and there, God knows, I play
With Venus' swans and sparrows all the day.
A dwarfish beldam bears me company,
That hops about the chamber where I lie,

And spends the night, that might be better spent,
In vain discourse and apish merriment—
Come thither." As she spake this, her tongue tripp'd,
For unawares, "Come thither," from her slipp'd ;
And suddenly her former colour chang'd,
And here and there her eyes through anger rang'd ;
And, like a planet moving several ways,
At one self instant, she, poor soul, assays,
Loving, not to love at all, and every part
Strove to resist the motions of her heart :
And hands so pure, so innocent, nay, such
As might have made Heaven stoop to have a touch,
Did she uphold to Venus, and again
Vow'd spotless chastity ; but all in vain ;
Cupid beats down her prayers with his wings ;
Her vows about the empty air he flings :
All deep enrag'd, his sinewy bow he bent,
And shot a shaft that burning from him went ;
Wherewith she strooken, look'd so dolefully,
As made Love sigh to see his tyranny ;
And, as she wept, her tears to pearl he turn'd,
And wound them on his arm, and for her mourn'd.
Then towards the palace of the Destinies,
Laden with languishment and grief, he flies,
And to those stern nymphs humbly made request,
Both might enjoy each other, and be blest.
But with a ghastly dreadful countenance,
Threatening a thousand deaths at every glance,
They answer'd Love, nor would vouchsafe so much
(M)

As one poor word, their hate to him was such :
Hearken a while, and I will tell you why.
   Heaven's winged herald, Jove-born Mercury,
The self-same day that he asleep had laid
Enchanted Argus, spied a country maid,
Whose careless hair, instead of pearl t'adorn it,
Glister'd with dew, as one that seemed to scorn it ;
Her breath as fragrant as the morning rose ;
Her mind pure, and her tongue untaught to glose ;
Yet proud she was (for lofty Pride that dwells
In towered courts, is oft in shepherds' cells),
And too-too well the fair vermilion knew
And silver tincture of her cheeks, that drew
The love of every swain.   On her this god
Enamour'd was, and with his snaky rod
Did charm her nimble feet, and made her stay,
The while upon a hillock down he lay,
And sweetly on his pipe began to play,
And with smooth speech her fancy to assay,
Till in his twining arms he lock'd her fast,
And then he woo'd with kisses ; and at last,
As shepherds do, her on the ground he laid,
And, tumbling in the grass, he often stray'd
Beyond the bounds of shame, in being bold
To eye those parts which no eye should behold ;
And, like an insolent commanding lover,
Boasting his parentage, would needs discover
The way to new Elysium.   But she,
Whose only dower was her chastity,

Having striven in vain, was now about to cry,
And crave the help of shepherds that were nigh.
Herewith he stay'd his fury, and began
To give her leave to rise : away she ran ;
After went Mercury, who used such cunning,
As she, to hear his tale, left off her running
(Maids are not won by brutish force and might,
But speeches full of pleasure and delight) ;
And, knowing Hermes courted her, was glad
That she such loveliness and beauty had
As could provoke his liking ; yet was mute,
And neither would deny nor grant his suit.
Still vow'd he love : she, wanting no excuse
To feed him with delays, as women use,
Or thirsting after immortality
(All women are ambitious naturally),
Impos'd upon her lover such a task,
As he ought not perform, nor yet she ask :
A draught of flowing nectar she requested
Wherewith the king of gods and men is feasted :
He, ready to accomplish what she will'd,
Stole some from Hebe (Hebe Jove's cup fill'd),
And gave it to his simple rustic love :
Which being known—as what is hid from Jove ?—
He inly storm'd, and wax'd more furious
Than for the fire filch'd by Prometheus ;
And thrust him down from heaven. He, wandering
    here,
In mournful terms, with sad and heavy cheer,

Complain'd to Cupid : Cupid, for his sake,
To be reveng'd on Jove did undertake ;
And those on whom heaven, earth, and hell relies,
I mean the adamantine Destinies,
He wounds with love, and forc'd them equally
To dote upon deceitful Mercury.
They offer'd him the deadly fatal knife
That shears the slender threads of human life ;
At his fair-feather'd feet the engines laid,
Which th' earth from ugly Chaos' den upweigh'd.
These he regarded not ; but did entreat
That Jove, usurper of his father's seat,
Might presently be banish'd into hell,
And agèd Saturn in Olympus dwell.
They granted what he crav'd ; and once again
Saturn and Ops began their golden reign :
Murder, rape, war, and lust, and treachery,
Were with Jove clos'd in Stygian empery.
But long this blessed time continu'd not :
As soon as he his wishèd purpose got,
He, reckless of his promise, did despise
The love of th' everlasting Destinies.
They, seeing it, both Love and him abhorr'd,
And Jupiter unto his place restor'd :
And, but that Learning, in despite of Fate,
Will mount aloft, and enter heaven-gate,
And to the seat of Jove itself advance,
Hermes had slept in hell with Ignorance.
Yet, as a punishment, they added this,

That he and Poverty should always kiss ;
And to this day is every scholar poor :
Gross gold from them runs headlong to the boor.
Likewise the angry Sisters, thus deluded,
To venge themselves on Hermes, have concluded
That Midas' brood shall sit in Honour's chair,
To which the Muses' sons are only heir ;
And fruitful wits, that inaspiring are,
Shall discontent run into regions far ;
And few great lords in virtuous deeds shall joy,
But be surpris'd with every garish toy,
And still enrich the lofty servile clown,
Who with encroaching guile keeps learning down.
Then muse not Cupid's suit no better sped,
Seeing in their loves the Fates were injurèd.

THE SECOND SESTIAD.

The Argument of the Second Sestiad.

Hero of love takes deeper sense,
And doth her love more recompense :
Their first night's meeting, where sweet kisses
Are th' only crowns of both their blisses :
He swims t' Abydos, and returns :
Cold Neptune with his beauty burns ;
Whose suit he shuns, and doth aspire
Hero's fair tower and his desire.

By this, sad Hero, with love unacquainted,
Viewing Leander's face, fell down and fainted.
He kiss'd her, and breath'd life into her lips ;

Wherewith, as one displeas'd, away she trips ;
Yet, as she went, full often look'd behind,
And many poor excuses did she find
To linger by the way, and once she stay'd,
And would have turn'd again, but was afraid,
In offering parley, to be counted light :
So on she goes, and, in her idle flight,
Her painted fan of curlèd plumes let fall,
Thinking to train Leander therewithal.
He, being a novice, knew not what she meant,
But stay'd, and after her a letter sent ;
Which joyful Hero answer'd in such sort,
As he had hope to scale the beauteous fort
Wherein the liberal Graces lock'd their wealth ;
And therefore to her tower he got by stealth.
Wide-open stood the door ; he need not climb ;
And she herself, before the 'pointed time,
Had spread the board, with roses strew'd the room,
And oft look'd out, and mus'd he did not come.
At last he came : O, who can tell the greeting
These greedy lovers had at their first meeting ?
He ask'd ; she gave ; and nothing was denied ;
Both to each other quickly were affied :
Look how their hands, so were their hearts united,
And what he did, she willingly requited.
(Sweet are the kisses, the embracements sweet,
When like desires and like affections meet ;
For from the earth to heaven is Cupid rais'd,
When fancy is in equal balance pais'd.)

Yet she this rashness suddenly repented,
And turn'd aside, and to herself lamented,
As if her name and honour had been wrong'd
By being possess'd of him for whom she long'd ;
Ay, and she wish'd, albeit not from her heart,
That he would leave her turret and depart.
The mirthful god of amorous pleasure smil'd
To see how he this captive nymph beguil'd ;
For hitherto he did but fan the fire,
And kept it down, that it might mount the higher.
Now wax'd she jealous lest his love abated,
Fearing her own thoughts made her to be hated.
Therefore unto him hastily she goes,
And, like light Salmacis, her body throws
Upon his bosom, where with yielding eyes
She offers up herself a sacrifice
To slake his anger, if he were displeas'd :
O, what god would not therewith be appeas'd ?
Like Æsop's cock, this jewel he enjoy'd,
And as a brother with his sister toy'd,
Supposing nothing else was to be done,
Now he her favour and goodwill had won.
But know you not that creatures wanting sense,
By nature have a mutual appetence,
And, wanting organs to advance a step,
Mov'd by love's force, unto each other lep ?
Much more in subjects having intellect
Some hidden influence breeds like effect.
Albeit Leander, rude in love and raw,

Long dallying with Hero, nothing saw
That might delight him more, yet he suspected
Some amorous rites or other were neglected.
Therefore unto his body hers he clung :
She, fearing on the rushes to be flung,
Striv'd with redoubled strength ; the more she striv'd,
The more a gentle pleasing heat reviv'd,
Which taught him all that elder lovers know ;
And now the same gan so to scorch and glow,
As in plain terms, yet cunningly, he crave it :
Love always makes those eloquent that have it.
She, with a kind of granting, put him by it,
And ever, as he thought himself most nigh it,
Like to the tree of Tantalus, she fled,
And, seeming lavish, sav'd her maidenhead.
Ne'er king more sought to keep his diadem,
Than Hero this inestimable gem :
Above our life we love a steadfast friend ;
Yet when a token of great worth we send,
We often kiss it, often look thereon,
And stay the messenger that would be gone ;
No marvel, then, though Hero would not yield
So soon to part from that she dearly held :
Jewels being lost are found again ; this never ;
'Tis lost but once, and once lost, lost for ever.

   Now had the Morn espied her lover's steeds ;
Whereat she starts, puts on her purple weeds,
And, red for anger that he stay'd so long,
All headlong throws herself the clouds among.

And now Leander, fearing to be miss'd,
Embrac'd her suddenly, took leave, and kiss'd :
Long was he taking leave, and loath to go,
And kiss'd again, as lovers use to do.
Sad Hero wrung him by the hand, and wept,
Saying, " Let your vows and promises be kept : "
Then standing at the door, she turned about,
As loath to see Leander going out.
And now the sun that through th' horizon peeps,
As pitying these lovers, downward creeps ;
So that in silence of the cloudy night,
Though it was morning, did he take his flight.
But what the secret trusty night conceal'd,
Leander's amorous habit soon reveal'd :
With Cupid's myrtle was his bonnet crown'd,
About his arms the purple riband wound,
Wherewith she wreath'd her largely-spreading hair ;
Nor could the youth abstain, but he must wear
The sacred ring wherewith she was endow'd,
When first religious chastity she vow'd ;
Which made his love through Sestos to be known,
And thence unto Abydos sooner blown
Than he could sail ; for incorporeal Fame,
Whose weight consists in nothing but her name,
Is swifter than the wind, whose tardy plumes
Are reeking water and dull earthly fumes.
    Home when he came, he seem'd not to be there,
But, like exiled air, thrust from his sphere,
Set in a foreign place ; and straight from thence,

Alcides-like, by mighty violence,
He would have chas'd away the swelling main,
That him from her unjustly did detain.
Like as the sun in a diameter
Fires and inflames objects removèd far,
And heateth kindly, shining laterally ;
So beauty sweetly quickens when 'tis nigh,
But being separated and remov'd,
Burns where it cherish'd, murders where it lov'd.
Therefore even as an index to a book,
So to his mind was young Leander's look.
Oh, none but gods have power their love to hide !
Affection by the countenance is descried ;
The light of hidden fire itself discovers,
And love that is conceal'd betrays poor lovers.
His secret flame apparently was seen :
Leander's father knew where he had been,
And for the same mildly rebuk'd his son,
Thinking to quench the sparkles new-begun.
But love resisted once, grows passionate,
And nothing more than counsel lovers hate ;
For as a hot proud horse highly disdains
To have his head controll'd, but breaks the reins,
Spits forth the ringled bit, and with his hoves
Checks the submissive ground ; so he that loves,
The more he is restrained, the worse he fares :
What is it now but mad Leander dares ?
"O Hero, Hero !" thus he cried full oft ;
And then he got him to a rock aloft,

Where having spied her tower, long star'd he on't,
And pray'd the narrow toiling Hellespont
To part in twain, that he might come and go ;
But still the rising billows answer'd, " No."
With that, he stripp'd him to the ivory skin,
And, crying " Love, I come," leap'd lively in :
Whereat the sapphire-visag'd god grew proud,
And made his capering Triton sound aloud,
Imagining that Ganymede, displeas'd,
Had left the heavens ; therefore on him he seized.
Leander striv'd ; the waves about him wound,
And pull'd him to the bottom, where the ground
Was strew'd with pearl, and in low coral groves
Sweet-singing mermaids sported with their loves
On heaps of heavy gold, and took great pleasure
To spurn in careless sort the shipwreck treasure ;
For here the stately azure palace stood,
Where kingly Neptune and his train abode.
The lusty god embrac'd him, call'd him "love,"
And swore he never should return to Jove :
But when he knew it was not Ganymed,
For under water he was almost dead,
He heav'd him up, and, looking on his face,
Beat down the bold waves with his triple mace,
Which mounted up, intending to have kiss'd him,
And fell in drops like tears because they miss'd him.
Leander, being up, began to swim,
And, looking back, saw Neptune follow him :
Whereat, aghast, the poor soul gan to cry,

"O, let me visit Hero ere I die ! "
The god put Helle's bracelet on his arm,
And swore the sea should never do him harm.
He clapp'd his plump cheeks, with his tresses play'd,
And, smiling wantonly, his love bewray'd ;
He watched his arms, and, as they open'd wide
At every stroke, betwixt them would he slide,
And steal a kiss, and then run out and dance,
And, as he turn'd, cast many a lustful glance,
And throw him gaudy toys to please his eye,
And dive into the water, and there pry
Upon his breast, his thighs, and every limb,
And up again, and close beside him swim,
And talk of love.   Leander made reply,
"You are deceiv'd ; I am no woman, I."
Thereat smil'd Neptune, and then told a tale,
How that a shepherd, sitting in a vale,
Play'd with a boy so lovely-fair and kind,
As for his love both earth and heaven pin'd ;
That of the cooling river durst not drink,
Lest water nymphs should pull him from the brink ;
And when he sported in the fragrant lawns,
Goat-footed Satyrs and up-staring Fauns
Would steal him thence.   Ere half this tale was done,
"Ay me," Leander cried, "th' enamour'd sun,
That now should shine on Thetis' glassy bower,
Descends upon my radiant Hero's tower :
O, that these tardy arms of mine were wings ! "
And, as he spake, upon the waves he springs.

Neptune was angry that he gave no ear,
And in his heart revenging malice bare :
He flung at him his mace ; but, as it went,
He call'd it in, for love made him repent :
The mace, returning back, his own hand hit,
As meaning to be veng'd for darting it.
When this fresh-bleeding wound Leander view'd,
His colour went and came, as if he ru'd
The grief which Neptune felt : in gentle breasts
Relentless thoughts, remorse, and pity rests ;
And who have hard hearts and obdurate minds,
But vicious, hare-brain'd, and illiterate hinds ?
The god, seeing him with pity to be mov'd,
Thereon concluded that he was belov'd
(Love is too full of faith, too credulous,
With folly and false hopes deluding us) ;
Wherefore, Leander's fancy to surprise,
To the rich ocean for gifts he flies :
'Tis wisdom to give much ; a gift prevails
When deep-persuading oratory fails.
    By this, Leander, being near the land,
Cast down his weary feet, and felt the sand.
Breathless albeit he were, he rested not
Till to the solitary tower he got ;
And knock'd, and call'd : at which celestial noise
The longing heart of Hero much more joys,
Than nymphs and shepherds when the timbrel rings,
Or crookèd dolphin when the sailor sings.
She stay'd not for her robes, but straight arose,

And, drunk with gladness, to the door she goes ;
Where seeing a naked man, she screech'd for fear
(Such sights as this to tender maids are rare),
And ran into the dark herself to hide
(Rich jewels in the dark are soonest spied).
Unto her was he led, or rather drawn,
By those white limbs which sparkled through th
   lawn.
And nearer that he came, the more she fled,
And, seeking refuge, slipt into her bed ;
Whereon Leander sitting, thus began,
Through numbing cold, all feeble, faint, and wan :
" If not for love, yet, love, for pity-sake,
Me in thy bed and maiden bosom take ;
At least vouchsafe these arms some little room,
Who, hoping to embrace thee, cheerly swoom :
This head was beat with many a churlish billow,
And therefore let it rest upon thy pillow."
Herewith affrighted, Hero shrunk away,
And in her lukewarm place Leander lay ;
Whose lively heat, like fire from heaven fet,
Would animate gross clay, and higher set
The drooping thoughts of base-declining souls,
Than dreary-Mars-carousing nectar bowls.
His hands he cast upon her like a snare :
She, overcome with shame and sallow fear,
Like chaste Diana when Actæon spied her,
Being suddenly betray'd, div'd down to hide her ;
And, as her silver body downward went,

With both her hands she made the bed a tent,
And in her own mind thought herself secure,
O'ercast with dim and darksome overture.
And now she lets him whisper in her ear,
Flatter, entreat, promise, protest, and swear :
Yet ever, as he greedily assay'd
To touch those dainties, she the harpy play'd,
And every limb did, as a soldier stout,
Defend the fort, and keep the foeman out ;
For though the rising ivory mount he scaled,
Which is with azure circling lines empal'd,
Much like a globe (a globe may I term this,
By which Love sails to regions full of bliss),
Yet there with Sisyphus he toil'd in vain,
The gentle parley did the truce obtain.
Even as a bird, which in our hands we wring,
Forth plungeth, and oft flutters with her wing,
She trembling strove : this strife of hers, like that
Which made the world, another world begat
Of unknown joy.   Treason was in her thought,
And cunningly to yield herself she sought.
Seeming not won, yet won she was at length :
In such wars women use but half their strength.
Leander now, like Theban Hercules,
Enter'd the orchard of the Hesperides ;
Whose fruit none rightly can describe, but he
That pulls or shakes it from the golden tree.
Wherein Leander, on her quivering breast,
Breathless spoke something, and sigh'd out the rest ;

Which so prevailed, as he, with small ado,
Enclos'd her in his arms, and kiss'd her too:
And every kiss to her was as a charm,
And to Leander as a fresh alarm :
So that the truce was broke, and she, alas,
Poor silly maiden, at his mercy was.
Love is not full of pity, as men say,
But deaf and cruel where he means to prey.
And now she wish'd this night were never done,
And sighed to think upon th' approaching sun ;
For much it griev'd her that the bright daylight
Should know the pleasure of this blessed night,
And them, like Mars and Erycine, display
Both in each other's arms chain'd as they lay.
Again, she knew not how to frame her look,
Or speak to him, who in a moment took
That which so long, so charily she kept ;
And fain by stealth away she would have crept,
And to some corner secretly have gone,
Leaving Leander in the bed alone.
But as her naked feet were whipping out,
He on the sudden cling'd her so about,
That mermaid-like, unto the floor she slid ;
One half appear'd, the other half was hid.
Thus near the bed she blushing stood upright,
And from her countenance behold ye might
A kind of twilight break, which through the air,
As from an orient cloud, glimps'd here and there ;
And round about the chamber this false morn

Brought forth the day before the day was born.
So Hero's ruddy cheek Hero betray'd,
And her all naked to his sight display'd :
Whence his admiring eyes more pleasure took
Than Dis, on heaps of gold fixing his look.
By this, Apollo's golden harp began
To sound forth music to the ocean ;
Which watchful Hesperus no sooner heard,
But he the bright Day-bearing car prepar'd,
And ran before, as harbinger of light,
And with his flaring beams mock'd ugly Night,
Till she o'ercome with anguish, shame, and rage,
Dang'd down to hell her loathsome carriage.

THE PASSIONATE SHEPHERD TO HIS LOVE.

COME live with me, and be my love ;
 And we will all the pleasures prove
That hills and valleys, dales and fields,
Woods or steepy mountain yields.

And we will sit upon the rocks,
Seeing the shepherds feed their flocks
By shallow rivers, to whose falls
Melodious birds sing madrigals.

And I will make thee beds of roses,
And a thousand fragrant posies ;
A cap of flowers, and a kirtle
Embroider'd all with leaves of myrtle ;

A gown made of the finest wool
Which from our pretty lambs we pull ;
Fair-lined slippers for the cold,
With buckles of the purest gold ;

A belt of straw and ivy-buds,
With coral clasps and amber studs :
An if these pleasures may thee move,
Come live with me, and be my love.

The shepherd-swains shall dance and sing
For thy delight each May morning :
If these delights thy mind may move,
Then live with me, and be my love.

FRAGMENT.

I WALK'D along a stream, for pureness rare,
  Brighter than sunshine ; for it did acquaint
The dullest sight with all the glorious prey
That in the pebble-pavèd channel lay.

No molten crystal, but a richer mine,
  Even Nature's rarest alchymy ran there—
Diamonds resolv'd, and substance more divine,
  Through whose bright-gliding current might
      appear
A thousand naked nymphs, whose ivory shine,
  Enamelling the banks, made them more dear
Than ever was that glorious palace gate
Where the day-shining Sun in triumph sate.

Upon this brim the eglantine and rose,
  The tamarisk, olive, and the almond tree,
As kind companions, in one union grows,
  Folding their twining arms, as oft we see
Turtle-taught lovers either other close,
  Lending to dulness feeling sympathy ;
And as a costly valance o'er a bed,
So did their garland-tops the brook o'erspread.

Their leaves, that differ'd both in shape and show,
  Though all were green, yet difference such in green,
Like to the checker'd bent of Iris' bow,
  Prided the running main, as it had been.

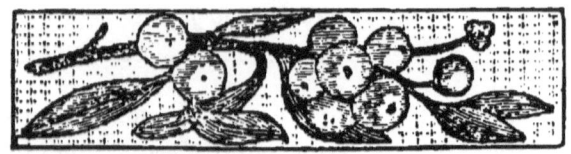

ELEGIES.

IN MORTEM PSITTACI.

THE parrot, from East India to me sent,
  Is dead : all fowls, her exequies frequent !
Go, godly birds, striking your breasts, bewail,
And with rough claws your tender cheeks assail.
For woful hairs let piece-torn plumes abound ;
For long shrild trumpets let your notes resound.
Why, Philomel, dost Tereus' lewdness mourn ?
All-wasting years have that complaint now worn :
Thy tunes let this rare bird's sad funeral borrow,
Itys a great, but ancient cause of sorrow.
All you whose pinions in the clear air soar,
But most, thou friendly turtle-dove, deplore :
Full concord all your lives was you betwixt,
And to the end your constant faith stood fixt ;
What Pylades did to Orestes prove,
Such to the parrot was the turtle-dove.
But what avail'd this faith ? her rarest hue ?
Or voice that how to change the wild notes knew ?

What helps it thou wert given to please my wench ?
Birds' hapless glory, death thy life doth quench.
Thou with thy quills mightst make green emeralds dark,
And pass our scarlet of red saffron's mark.
No such voice-feigning bird was on the ground ;
Thou spok'st thy words so well with stammering sound.
Envy hath rapt thee : no fierce wars thou mov'd'st ;
Vain-babbling speech and pleasant peace thou lov'd'st.
Behold, how quails among their battles live !
Which do perchance old age unto them give.
A little fill'd thee ; and, for love of talk,
Thy mouth to taste of many meats did balk.
Nuts were thy food, and poppy caus'd thee sleep ;
Pure water's moisture thirst away did keep.
The ravenous vulture lives ; the puttock hovers
Around the air ; the cadess rain discovers ;
And crow survives arms-bearing Pallas' hate,
Whose life nine ages scarce bring out of date.
Dead is that speaking image of man's voice,
The parrot given me, the far world's best choice.
The greedy spirits take the best things first,
Supplying their void places with the worst.
Thersites did Protesilaus survive ;
And Hector died, his brothers yet alive.
My wench's vows for thee what should I show,
Which stormy south winds into sea did blow ?
The seventh day came ; none following mightst thou
   see ;
And the Fate's distaff empty stood to thee.

Yet words in thy benummèd palate rung ;
" Farewell, Corinna," cried thy dying tongue.
Elysium hath a wood of holm trees black,
Whose earth doth not perpetual green grass lack.
There good birds rest (if we believe things hidden),
Whence unclean fowls are said to be forbidden.
There harmless swans feed all abroad the river ;
There lives the phœnix, one alone bird ever ;
There Juno's bird displays his gorgeous feather,
And loving doves kiss eagerly together.
The parrot, into wood receiv'd with these,
Turns all the godly birds to what she please.
A grave her bones hides : on her corps' great grave,
The little stones these little verses have—
This tomb approves I pleas'd my mistress well ;
My mouth in speaking did all birds excel.

AD AMNEM, DUM ITER FACERET AD AMICAM.

FLOOD with reed-grown slime banks, till I be past,
Thy waters stay ; I to my mistress hast.
Thou hast no bridge, nor boat with ropes to throw,
That may transport me, without oars to row.
Thee I have pass'd, and knew thy stream none such,
When thy wave's brim did scarce my ankles touch.
With snow thaw'd from the next hill now thou gushest,
And in thy foul deep waters thick thou rushest.

What helps my haste ? what to have ta'en small
   rest ?
What day and night to travel in her quest ?
If, standing here, I can by no means get
My foot upon the further bank to set.
Now wish I those wings noble Perseus had,
Bearing the head with dreadful adders clad ;
Now wish the chariot whence corn-fields were found
First to be thrown upon the untill'd ground :
I speak old poets' wonderful inventions ;
Ne'er was, nor [e'er] shall be, what my verse mentions.
Rather, thou large bank-overflowing river,
Slide in thy bounds ; so shalt thou run for ever.
Trust me, land-stream, thou shalt no envy lack,
If I a lover be by thee held back.
Great floods ought to assist young men in love ;
Great floods the force of it do often prove.
In mid Bithynia, 'tis said, Inachus
Grew pale, and, in cold fords, hot lecherous.
Troy had not yet been ten years' siege' outstander,
When nymph Neæra rapt thy looks, Scamander.
What, not Alpheus in strange lands to run,
Th' Arcadian virgin's constant love hath won ?
And Crusa unto Xanthus first affied,
They say, Peneus near Phthia's town did hide.
What should I name Asop, that Thebe lov'd,
Thebe, who mother of five daughters prov'd ?
If, Achelöus, I ask where thy horns stand,
Thou say'st, broke with Alcides' angry hand.

Not Calydon nor Ætolia did please ;
One Deïanira was more worth than these.
Rich Nile, by seven mouths to the vast sea flowing,
Who so well keeps his water's head from knowing,
Is by Evadne thought to take such flame,
As his deep whirlpools could not quench the same.
Dry Enipeus, Tyro to embrace,
Fly back his stream charg'd ; the stream charg'd, gave
　　place.
Nor pass I thee, who hollow rocks down tumbling,
In Tibur's field with watery foam art rumbling ;
Whom Ilia pleas'd, though in her looks grief revell'd,
Her cheeks were scratch'd, her goodly hairs dishevell'd.
She, wailing Mars' sin and her uncle's crime,
Stray'd barefoot through sole places on a time.
Her, from his swift waves, the bold flood perceiv'd,
And from the mid ford his hoarse voice upheav'd,
Saying, " Why sadly tread'st my banks upon,
Ilia, sprung from Idæan Laomedon ?
Where's thy attire ? why wander'st here alone ?
To stay thy tresses white veil hast thou none ?
Why weep'st, and spoil'st with tears thy watery eyes ?
And fiercely knock'st thy breast that open lies ?
His heart consists of flint and hardest steel,
That, seeing thy tears, can any joy then feel.
Fear not : to thee our court stands open wide ;
There shalt be lov'd : Ilia, lay fear aside.
Thou o'er a hundred nymphs or more shalt reign,
For five-score nymphs or more our floods contain.

Nor, Roman stock, scorn me so much, I crave :
Gifts than my promise greater thou shalt have."
This said he. She her modest eyes held down ;
Her woful bosom a warm shower did drown.
Thrice she prepar'd to fly, thrice she did stay,
By fear depriv'd of strength to run away.
Yet, rending with enragèd thumb her tresses,
Her trembling mouth these unmeet sounds expresses :
" O, would in my forefathers' tomb deep laid
My bones had been, while yet I was a maid !
Why, being a vestal, am I woo'd to wed,
Deflower'd and stainèd in unlawful bed ?
Why stay I ? men point at me for a whore ;
Shame, that should make me blush, I have no more."
This said, her coat hoodwink'd her fearful eyes,
And into water desperately she flies.
'Tis said the slippery stream held up her breast,
And kindly gave her what she likèd best.
And I believe some wench thou hast affected ;
But woods and groves keep your faults undetected.
While thus I speak, the waters more abounded,
And from the channel all abroad surrounded.
Mad stream, why dost our mutual joys defer ?
Clown, from my journey why dost me deter ?
How wouldst thou flow, wert thou a noble flood ?
If thy great fame in every region stood ?
Thou hast no name, but com'st from snowy mountains ;
No certain house thou hast, nor any fountains ;
Thy springs are naught but rain and melted snow,

Which wealth cold winter doth on thee bestow.
Either thou'rt muddy in mid-winter tide,
Or, full of dust, dost on the dry earth slide.
What thirsty traveller ever drunk of thee ?
Who said with grateful voice, " Perpetual be ? "
Harmful to beasts and to the fields thou proves :
Perchance these others, me mine own loss moves.
To this I fondly loves of floods told plainly ;
I shame so great names to have us'd so vainly.
I know not what expecting, I erewhile
Nam'd Achelöus, Inachus, and Nile.
But for thy merits I wish thee, white stream,
Dry winters aye, and suns in heat extreme.

TIBULLI MORTEM DEFLET.

If Thetis and the Morn their sons did wail,
And envious Fates great goddesses assail,
Sad Elegy, thy woful hairs unbind :
Ah, now a name too true thou hast I find !
Tibullus, thy work's poet, and thy fame,
Burns his dead body in the funeral flame.
Lo, Cupid brings his quiver spoilèd quite,
His broken bow, his firebrand without light !
How piteously with drooping wings he stands,
And knocks his bare breast with self-angry hands !
The locks spread on his neck receive his tears,
And shaking sobs his mouth for speeches bears :

So at Æneas' burial, men report,
Fair-fac'd Iülus, he went forth thy court:
And Venus' grieves, Tibullus' life being spent,
As when the wild boar Adon's groin had rent.
The gods' care we are call'd, and men of piety,
And some there be that think we have a deity.
Outrageous death profanes all holy things,
And on all creatures obscure darkness brings.
To Thracian Orpheus what did parents good,
Or songs amazing wild beasts of the wood?
Where Linus, by his father Phœbus laid,
To sing with his unequall'd harp is said.
See, Homer, from whose fountain ever fill'd
Pierian dew to poets is distill'd!
Him the last day in black Avern hath drown'd:
Verses alone are with continuance crown'd.
The work of poets lasts; Troy's labour's fame,
And that slow web night's falsehood did unframe.
So Nemesis, so Delia famous are;
The one his first love, th' other his new care.
What profit to us hath our pure life bred?
What to have lain alone in empty bed?
When bad Fates take good men, I am forbod
By secret thoughts to think there is a god.
Live godly, thou shalt die; though honour heaven,
Yet shall thy life be forcibly bereaven:
Trust in good verse, Tibullus feels death's pains;
Scarce rests of all what a small urn contains.
Thee, sacred poet, could sad flames destroy?

Nor fearèd they thy body to annoy ?
The holy gods' gilt temples they might fire,
That durst to so great wickedness aspire.
Eryx' bright empress turn'd her looks aside,
And some, that she refrain'd tears, have denied.
Yet better is't, than if Corcyra's isle
Had thee unknown interr'd in ground most vile.
Thy dying eyes here did thy mother close,
Nor did thy ashes her last offerings lose.
Part of her sorrow here thy sister bearing,
Comes forth, her unkemb'd locks asunder tearing.
Nemesis and thy first wench join their kisses
With thine, nor this last fire their presence misses.
Delia departing, ''Happier lov'd,'' she saith,
''Was I : thou liv'dst, while thou esteem'd'st my
    faith.''
Nemesis answers, '' What's my loss to thee ?
His fainting hand in death engraspèd me.''
If aught remains of us but name and spirit,
Tibullus doth Elysium's joy inherit.
Their youthful brows with ivy girt, to meet him,
With Calvus, learn'd Catullus comes and greet him ;
And thou, if falsely charg'd to wrong thy friend,
Gallus, that car'd'st not blood and life to spend.
With these thy soul walks, souls if death release :
The godly sweet Tibullus doth increase.
Thy bones, I pray, may in the urn safe rest,
And may th' earth's weight thy ashes naught molest !

DELIBERATIO POETÆ, UTRUM ELEGOS PERGAT SCRIBERE

AN POTIUS TRAGŒDIAS.

An old wood stands, uncut of long years' space:
'Tis credible some god-head haunts the place ;
In midst thereof a stone-pav'd sacred spring,
Where round about small birds most sweetly sing.
Here while I walk, hid close in shady grove,
To find what work my Muse might move, I strove,
Elegia came with hairs perfumèd sweet,
And one, I think, was longer, of her feet :
A decent form, thin robe, a lover's look ;
By her foot's blemish greater grace she took.
Then with huge steps came violent Tragedy :
Stern was her front, her cloak on ground did lie ;
Her left hand held abroad a regal sceptre ;
The Lydian buskin in fit paces kept her.
And first she said, " When will thy love be spent,
O poet careless of thy argument ?
Wine-bibbing banquets tell thy naughtiness,
Each cross-way's corner doth as much express.
Oft some points at the prophet passing by,
And ' this is he whom fierce love burns,' they cry.
A laughing stock thou art to all the city,
While without shame thou sing'st thy lewdness ditty.
'Tis time to move grave things in lofty style ;
Long hast thou loiter'd ; greater works compile.
The subject hides thy wit : men's acts resound ;

This thou wilt say to be a worthy ground.
Thy Muse hath play'd what may mild girls content,
And by those numbers is thy first youth spent.
Now give the Roman Tragedy a name ;
To fill my laws thy wanton spirit frame."
This said, she mov'd her buskins gaily varnish'd,
And seven times shook her head with thick locks
    garnish'd.
The other smiled (I wot) with wanton eyes:
Err I, or myrtle in her right hand lies ?
" With lofty words, stout Tragedy," she said,
" Why treadest me down ? art thou aye gravely play'd ?
Thou deign'st unequal lines should thee rehearse ;
Thou fight'st against me, using mine own verse.
Thy lofty style with mine I not compare :
Small doors unfitting for large houses are.
Light am I, and with me, my care, light Love ;
Not stronger am I than the thing I move.
Venus without me should be rustical ;
This goddess' company doth to me befal.
What gate thy stately words cannot unlock,
My flattering speeches soon wide-open knock.
And I deserve more than thou canst in verity,
By suffering much not borne by thy severity.
By me Corinna learns, cozening her guard,
To get the door with little noise unbarr'd ;
And slipp'd from bed, cloth'd in a loose night-gown,
To move her feet unheard in setting down.
Ah, how oft on hard doors hung I engrav'd,

From no man's reading fearing to be sav'd !
But, till the keeper went forth, I forget not,
The maid to hide me in her bosom let not.
What gift with me was on her birthday sent,
But cruelly by her was drown'd and rent ;
First of thy mind the happy seeds I knew ;
Thou hast my gift, which she would from thee sue."
She left.   I said, " You both I must beseech,
To empty air may go my fearful speech.
With sceptres and high buskins th' one would dress me ;
So through the world should bright renown express me.
The other gives my love a conquering name ;
Come, therefore, and to long verse shorter frame.
Grant, Tragedy, thy poet time's least tittle :
Thy labour ever lasts ; she asks but little."
She gave me leave.   Soft loves, in time make hast ;
Some greater work will urge me on at last.

www.ingramcontent.com/pod-product-compliance
Lightning Source LLC
Chambersburg PA
CBHW020001030726

47500CB00002B/388